JACK'S RUN

Other Novels by Roland Smith

JACK'S RUN

roland smith

Hyperion Paperbacks for Children
New York

First Hyperion Paperbacks edition, 2007
1 3 5 7 9 10 8 6 4 2
Printed in the United States of America
ISBN-13: 978-1-4231-0407-0
ISBN-10: 1-4231-0407-2
Library of Congress Cataloging-in-Publication Data on file.

Visit www.hyperionbooksforchildren.com

For all of those who wrote and asked:
"What happens next?"

Dear Catalin,

This is the letter I wanted to send to you, but couldn't. . . .

My real name is Jack Osborne. A year ago my dad was arrested and put in jail for drug trafficking. Three men broke into our house and threatened to kill my sister, my mom, and me, if my dad didn't keep his mouth shut about the drug cartel he was flying for. The head of the cartel is a man named Alonzo Aznar. He was one of the three men who broke into our house that horrible night.

Dad told the Drug Enforcement Agency he would give them all the information they needed to take Alonzo down in exchange for keeping us safe. When Dad worked for Alonzo he kept a diary detailing every aspect of Alonzo's drug operation.

Our names were changed, we were put into the Witness Security Program run by the U.S. Marshal Service, and sent to Elko, Nevada, to start a new life.

As you know, Alonzo Aznar found us in Elko. Thanks to Sam Sebesta, Alonzo is in jail now, awaiting trial, but our problems aren't over. He still has people out looking for us and Dad's diary.

We're the Greenes now. Robert and Melanie, and their two kids—Christine and Mack.

Not a day goes by when I don't think of you, Cat. My biggest fear is not Alonzo Aznar. It's the possibility that I'll never see you again.

I can't send this letter to you yet. But one day, when it's safe, I'll put a stamp in the upper right-hand corner and give it to the postman. That will be the happiest day of my life.

Love,

Jack

Day One

THE
GREENES

1

The phone rang, but Mack did not get up to answer it.

He was lying in bed, a breeze was blowing through the screened-in porch, and he was feeling comfortable for the first time in twenty-four hours. It wasn't so much the heat that bothered him in Manteo, it was the humidity—sticky, cloying, like swimming through warm chicken broth.

The Greenes had moved to Manteo in November. The weather was fine throughout winter and spring, but when school let out in June, the heat wrapped Roanoke Island in a shroud of perpetual humidity. The only relief came between five and eight o'clock in the morning, when an Atlantic breeze blew in from the Outer Banks. The best place to catch the breeze was the screened-in porch overlooking their backyard.

At first Mack's mother was not thrilled with the idea of her son sleeping on the porch. "Not enough security," she insisted. "Too dangerous." But after a couple weeks of Mack's complaining, she gave in.

The phone continued to ring. They had an answering machine, but his father had forgotten to switch it on when he left for work.

Whoever was calling wanted to talk to someone, but Mack knew that someone was not him. He had been in Manteo eight months and still didn't know anyone well enough to give them the family's unlisted phone number.

The last time he had made a friend, she had nearly been killed. He figured he would have plenty of time for friends in the fall when he started eighth grade. By then he would know the fate of Alonzo Aznar. He would know if it was safe.

The phone was still ringing. He sat up and looked at his watch. Five after eight.

He knew it wasn't his mother. She and Christine were in Los Angeles, which was three hours behind East Coast time, and neither one of them were early risers. It wouldn't be one of his father's customers with a leaky toilet or broken windowpane either. He used his cell phone for his handyman calls.

But it could be Dad trying to reach me, he thought, swinging his legs out of bed. He knows there isn't a chance in a million I'll have my cell phone turned on.

Mack didn't even know where his cell phone was, or if the battery was charged. There was no point in carrying a cell phone if you didn't have anyone to call.

He walked into the kitchen and picked up the phone.

"Hello, Mack?"

It was Doris Welty.

"I didn't wake you, did I?"

"Kind of," he said.

"So, how's everything going?"

"Good."

Doris was a U.S. Marshal. She and her partner, Donald Smites, were their handlers. It was their job to protect the Greenes of Manteo, North Carolina, which had not worked out very well when they were the Grangers of Elko, Nevada.

"No bad guys hanging around?" she asked. "People giving off weird vibes? Any funny feelings?"

Mack had plenty of funny feelings these days, but he wasn't about to share them with Doris.

"Sixth sense stuff?" she asked.

She and Don were constantly talking about the sixth sense stuff. "If you think you're being followed or watched," Don had told him, "you probably are."

"No," Mack said. "No sixth sense." The truth was, he didn't have this sense that they were always harping about.

"I understand you and your dad are batching it," Doris said.

"Right," Mack verified, seeing that his father had left him a note on the counter.

I'll pick you up at six for some blue crab at the beach.
Dad

"How's your dad's business?" Doris asked.

"Good. How's Don?"

"He's on vacation," Doris answered. "Speaking of which, what are you doing this summer?"

"Helping Dad a couple days a week. Hanging around. I might spend some time with Christine in Los Angeles before school." Unless I can talk my parents out of it, he thought.

"Your mom and sister are having a ball in L.A.," Doris said. "I talked to them last night."

Mack understood now. This was an official call. Doris was letting him know that she was keeping tabs on them. The marshals were not the only ones doing this. Agent Pelton, the drug enforcement agent who had arrested his father, called once or twice a week. So did the prosecuting attorneys who were trying to convict Alonzo Aznar. The calls were patched through the marshals' office in Washington, D.C. No one but Doris and Don knew where the Osbornes were living or who they had become.

"What's going on with Alonzo?" he asked.

The question was followed by a long pause. Mack knew that Doris was not comfortable discussing Alonzo with him, which is exactly why he asked the question.

"Oh," she said finally. "You don't need to worry about him anymore."

Mack rolled his eyes and was tempted to tell her that if that was the case, why were the Greenes in the Witness Security Program? "That's not what I meant," he said. "Is the trial on schedule?"

"I'm a marshal, not a federal prosecutor," she said. "You should ask your dad about that."

Mack glanced at the calendar on the refrigerator. There was a red question mark on Wednesday, the week after next, and a red line drawn through the next several weeks. He had noticed them for the first time the night before.

8

"We've talked about it," he said, which wasn't even close to the truth. "The trial starts in a couple weeks."

Again, Doris hesitated then said, "Really?"

Mack was not the only one fiddling with the truth. The same date was marked on Doris's desk calendar.

"We were wondering if it's going to be delayed again," he said, as if he and his father had talked about it just that morning over breakfast.

"I don't think so," Doris said, giving in. "Wednesday is the start of all the pretrial stuff. Arguments, preliminary motions, jury selection . . . things like that. Your dad's part won't start for a while."

"Why did the trial get delayed so many times?" Mack asked. "It seems to me that Alonzo would want to try to get out of jail as quick as he can."

"First of all, Mack, he's not going to get out. He and his attorneys know this. Right now he's being kept in a federal holding facility in Atlanta, Georgia, which is posh compared to where he will be sent once he's convicted. As the accused, Alonzo is afforded certain comforts that aren't available inside a federal penitentiary. He's delaying the inevitable, but his time is just about up."

Mack sat down at the table, happy now that he had decided to answer the phone. In ten minutes he had learned more about what was going on with Alonzo Aznar than he had in the previous eight months. His parents refused to talk about Alonzo with Mack and his sister, Christine. Their reasoning was that they wanted them to forget about what had happened, or what might happen, and concentrate on being the Greene kids from Manteo, North Carolina.

Christine—the actress—had no problem with this. She had made a pile of new friends, and finished her senior year in high school "without a hitch," as his mother proudly put it. Playing Christine Greene was just another acting role for her.

For Mack, the adjustment had not been quite so smooth. He'd had a few "hitches." He could not quite forget that Alonzo Aznar had tried to kill him twice. And he couldn't stop wondering what had happened to Sam Sebesta, the custodian and former Russian spy who had saved his life. Or Catalin Cristobal—especially Cat—who he had not even had a chance to talk to before they left Elko.

What does Cat think of me now? he thought for the thousandth time. What do her parents think of me? Will I be able to talk to her after this is all over?

Mack and Catalin's relationship had just gotten started when Alonzo came to Elko looking for his father's diary. Alonzo had kidnapped Catalin and threatened to kill her if Mack didn't turn it over to him.

"Mack?" Doris said. "Are you there?"

"Uh . . . yeah . . . sorry."

Doris laughed. "I'll let you go. I just called to check in and see how you're doing."

"Wait," he said. "I have a couple more questions. Have you heard from Sam?"

"Who?"

"Sam Sebesta."

"The custodian?"

Right, he thought. Sam is no more a custodian than you are, Doris. He had not only captured Alonzo in Elko, he had also saved the diary, which was the only thing that was keeping his father out of jail.

"Yeah," Mack said. "The guy who caught Alonzo and saved my life."

"No," Doris said. "There would be no reason for him to get in touch with us. Why?"

"I was just wondering. I mean, after what he did to Alonzo . . . I guess I'm just worried about him."

"I'm sure Alonzo has more important things to think about than the custodian at your old school."

"What about Catalin?" he asked. "Did she ever write me back?" After they'd left Elko, the marshals allowed him to write a letter to her, censored of course, and nothing like the letter he really wanted to send.

"Mack," Doris said gently. "The Osbornes and the Grangers have no return address. I know it's hard, but you really need to forget about what happened in Elko and before. You need to move on with the life you have now."

The problem is, Mack thought, I can't. I left my life back in Elko with Catalin Cristobal. But he couldn't tell Doris that—he couldn't tell anybody.

2

Christine Greene was beautiful, outgoing, talented, and, like her father, able to make friends wherever she happened to be. Los Angeles, California, was no exception.

On the flight to the West Coast, she met a successful screenwriter, and a documentary producer. Both of them had given her their phone numbers, with a promise to help her if she needed anything.

She and her mother thought it would take two or three weeks to find a place for her to live, but it only took two days. It turned out that the screenwriter she'd met knew someone who knew someone who lived near the university and was looking for a roommate. Hannah Vernon was an aspiring actress like Christine, but a few years older. They hit it off as soon as they met, and the next day Christine and her mother moved into Hannah's three-bedroom bungalow on a quiet street with a lemon tree in the backyard.

Finding a place so quickly was a huge relief for Melanie Greene. She wanted her daughter to be completely settled before Mack came out to stay. The prosecutors had predicted the trial could last for weeks, perhaps months. During that time, the Greenes would be very exposed. Alonzo's people would know where they were.

"I don't think he'd try anything," Agent Pelton had said. "But you never know with Alonzo. He's nuts. If he goes to prison, he has nothing to lose. It would be best to keep the kids out of the picture, with someone you trust."

There were plenty of people they trusted when they were the Osbornes—family members, old friends—but the Greenes had no family and no close friends. And even if there were someone to watch the kids, what would Melanie tell them? *Thanks for taking the children. By the way, keep a close eye out for homicidal drug dealers. If they get in your house they'll kill everyone there.* No, the only solution was to send Mack to stay with his sister.

Mack would arrive in L.A. just before the trial. They hadn't told him yet that his stay would be longer than he expected. Mack had grown a little unpredictable after Elko, and Melanie didn't know how he would react to the news. He was no longer her easygoing son of the year before.

The first thing he had asked for when they got to Manteo was exercise equipment and a place to work out. Before this, exercise was something they had to force him to do. He would much rather have had a book in his hands than a barbell.

He approached his workouts with almost a religious fervor—never missing a day, even when he was sick. He had always been tall for his age, but now with the weight training he was "way buff," as Christine would say. Melanie hardly recognized him anymore, but the change went deeper than muscle tone. Before Elko, she always knew where she stood with Mack, because he would tell you in very plain English. Since moving to Manteo, he had become a lot more reserved, speaking up only when asked a specific question, and sometimes not even then.

In spite of finding a place for Christine quickly, Melanie still had a lot to do. They had to register Christine at UCLA, where she was going to major in film with a minor in music. They had to buy an inexpensive car for her to get around in. They had to enroll at a health club so Mack could continue his workouts. And the final chore was to check out the local schools for Mack, in case the trial continued into the fall, which she hoped would not be the case.

The morning before she was to leave for Manteo, Melanie sat in the bungalow's kitchen with Christine, eating what might be their last meal alone together for some time. Hannah was out running errands, which allowed them to speak freely, something they couldn't do when Hannah was there.

"Are you sure you're all right with Mack's coming out here?" she asked.

"Where else can you send him?" Christine said. "Besides, I don't mind having him here. We get along . . . most of the time. And Hannah thinks it will be fun. She has a little brother back in Ohio about Mack's age. She misses him."

"Even if the trial goes on longer than expected?" Melanie

14

asked. "You'll have to get him enrolled in school. Make sure he gets his homework done, drive him around, enforce curfews. . . ."

Christine laughed. "Knowing Mack, he'll be trying to enforce a curfew on me, and make me do *my* homework. Don't worry. Between Hannah and me, we'll be able to handle Mack. In fact, he might even like it out here."

"I hope you're right."

"Have you told him about the plan?"

"Not exactly," Melanie said. "I mean, he knows he's coming out here, but we haven't told him his stay may be longer than he thinks. I spoke with Dad last night and he promised to tell him over dinner tonight."

"He's not going to be happy," Christine said.

"I know." Robert had told Melanie something else during their phone conversation, and now seemed like the best time to tell Christine. "If I can get a flight," she said. "I'm going to head back to Manteo tomorrow."

"Tomorrow?" Christine said, surprised. "I thought the trial wasn't for a couple weeks."

"It's not," Melanie said. "At least our part. But one of the prosecutors called, along with Agent Pelton, and said that we might have to get down to Georgia early to help with pretrial motions. They want us close by in case they need us." She hesitated. "I think, and this is totally up to you, it would be best for Mack to come out here as soon as possible. That way your dad and I can have a few days to get ready without worrying about what to do with Mack."

"When?" Christine asked.

"Again, it's totally your decision, but the easiest thing

15

for us would be to put him on an outbound flight when I fly into Norfolk. It would save us four or five hours getting him back up to the airport. But if you need more time to get settled here, we'll understand."

Christine thought about it for a moment, then shook her head. "Send him out," she said. "The only thing you and Dad need to worry about is making sure that Alonzo Aznar goes to prison forever."

3

Alonzo Aznar had no intention of going to prison forever.

He had been in a federal holding facility in Atlanta for the past eight months. As far as jails went, it wasn't bad, but he was eager to get out.

This was not his first experience behind bars. When he was a young man he had been sent to prison in Colombia. It was nothing like this American jail. The men here considered themselves dangerous men, but they were puppies compared to the hungry wolves he had shared the crowded cells with as a youth.

It had taken him less than two days to establish himself at the top of the pecking order in his cell block, and he didn't have to use violence to achieve it. Instead, he used his wealth and power on the two swaggering inmates in charge of the others.

"All I want is to be left alone," he told them. "No hassles.

I have much work to do while I'm here. I need you two to watch my back twenty-four hours a day, seven days a week, making certain that no one bothers me."

"What do we get?"

"Money, of course," Alonzo said. "More than you ever managed to steal on the outside."

"And if we refuse?"

Alonzo flashed a white smile at them. "Then you will be killed, as will everyone you have ever been close to." He pushed two sheets of paper across the table. One for each man. On them were the names of girlfriends, wives, parents, children, brothers, and sisters. The two men read over the lists in shock.

"You may keep the lists," Alonzo said. "The addresses are current. Perhaps you would like to contact some of these people."

The arrangement had worked out well. With a little more money to the guards, he had a cell to himself, a television, and he was allowed to keep his small, handheld wireless computer. The handheld was his lifeline to the outside, the only thing keeping his organization from falling apart. He had paid a great deal of money for the system. All of his key people carried identical units. The computer was equipped with an unbreakable encryption program. When an e-mail was sent, the recipient had only a few minutes to answer after opening it before the e-mail and reply address were permanently destroyed. This way, there was no record of the e-mail left on the computers, and the e-mails could not be traced.

* * *

Alonzo sat on the cot in his small cell, composing the last e-mail of the morning, when a guard appeared in his doorway.

"Your attorney is here."

Alonzo followed the guard down the long corridor, through several locked doors, to the interview room. The well-fed Benjamin Bender was sitting at the table in his expensive three-piece suit, his alligator-skin briefcase open in front of him.

Bender had a very large and successful law practice, but only one client really mattered. That client was standing in front of him now, wearing an orange jumpsuit. Bender got to his feet and held out his beefy hand.

Alonzo declined to take it and sat. "Did you get the trial delayed?"

Bender shook his head.

"I need more time." Alonzo said.

"There's nothing I can do." Bender ran a finger under the starched collar of his white shirt. "We were lucky to get it delayed as long as we did."

Alonzo was irritated, but not surprised. He had expected this. "And Osborne's diary?"

Again, Bender shook his head. "No sign of it. I don't think the prosecutors have it."

This was better news. Alonzo had never seen the diary—in fact, he had been arrested trying to retrieve it from the boy—but it supposedly detailed every aspect of his vast drug cartel. If the Drug Enforcement Agency got a hold of it, that would be the end of everything.

"Are you certain they don't have it?" Alonzo asked quietly.

"Yes," Bender answered. "The prosecution has to disclose all the evidence they have against you so we can prepare our defense. There's been no mention of the diary. If they had it, we would know."

"Why would Neil hold it back?"

"Leverage against the DEA perhaps," Bender speculated. "Remember, Neil was in jail, too, but they cut him loose to be with his family. That's very unusual. Normally, they would have kept him locked up tight until the trial was over. Made him earn his freedom. I wouldn't concern yourself about the diary. It's Neil's testimony at your trial, and the information he's already given them, that we have to worry about. Neil's testimony is the key to the case they have against you." Bender paused, then said, "Getting him to change his story would be very helpful."

"Unfortunately," Alonzo said tightly, "we have not been able to find him to discuss this, which is why I need more time."

"There's nothing I can do," Bender repeated helplessly.

Alonzo gave him an ice-cold stare. "But there are many things that I can do, even from a prison cell, if this doesn't come out in a favorable way. I have paid you a great deal of money over the years. Now you must earn that money. Do not let me down."

Bender was visibly sweating. He knew that Alonzo was having him followed, and he suspected that his office and home had been bugged. If he failed, there would be no escape. Taking Alonzo Aznar on as a client had been the biggest mistake of his life.

"I have some other news," Bender said nervously.

"I'm listening."

"They've offered you a plea bargain."

"Go on."

"Fifteen years," Bender said. "You could be out in five. Maybe less."

In five years Alonzo's operation would be gone. In fact, if he didn't get out in the next few weeks, all would be lost. "You're not suggesting I take their offer."

"Of course not," Bender said, without much conviction. "But by law I have to run it by you."

"You will tell them that I have declined their offer," Alonzo said.

4

When Alonzo had found the Grangers in Elko, Mack's father was still in jail.

Neil Osborne had made a deal with Agent Pelton of the DEA. He would give them all the information they needed to convict Alonzo if they put his family in the Witness Security Program and guaranteed their safety. The deal did not include a get-out-of-jail-free card. As Neil had told Mack just before the family left for Elko: "It's easy to have regrets after you've been caught. I deserve to be in prison. What I did was wrong. I gave up everything I loved and nearly got you all killed. I can't undo what I've done, but as soon as you're safe, I'm going to do everything in my power to break up this cartel. I'm going to tell them what I know so I can live with myself. I'm going to tell them because it's the right thing to do."

But Mack's father's commitment to the DEA shifted after

Alonzo found the family. Neil threatened to back out of the deal unless they let him out to protect his family personally. Reluctantly, the authorities went along with him, but there were restrictions. They took his passport and his pilot's license away. They gave him a special cell phone that he had to carry with him at all times. Inside the phone was a homing device hooked up to a computer that kept track of every step he took throughout the day. If it didn't like where he was or where he was headed, it sent a page to Don or Doris. One of them would call and ask him what he was up to. If he didn't answer the phone, or they didn't like his answer, a federal warrant would be issued for his immediate arrest.

In addition to this, the computer made random calls to the cell phone. When he answered, it would give him a series of words to repeat. If the computer didn't recognize his voice print, an alert would go out. It rang at all hours, day and night, but he thought it a small price to pay to be back with his family.

The marshals found a three-bedroom brick ranch house for the Greenes, on a quiet street at the edge of Manteo. It was much better than the matchbox they had stuffed them into in Elko. The first improvement Mack's father made was to install a sophisticated security system. The second improvement was to hide a knife, pistol, or shotgun in every room in the house, including the two bathrooms. In their former lives, Mack's mother would have never allowed a weapon of any kind in their house. Things had changed, though. She didn't even let out a whimper of protest over the guns, and dutifully went with them across the bridge to the Alligator River Refuge for several weekends to undergo what his father called, "Small arms combat training."

This is when Mack found out that his father had been a Navy SEAL before he'd become a naval fighter pilot. SEALs handle classified missions from sea, air, or land, which is where the acronym comes from. Their missions include reconnaissance, clandestine operations, and unconventional counter-guerilla warfare. Very few people are picked to undergo SEAL training, and of those, only a few make it through to become operators. Mack's father not only became an operator, he went on to become a SEAL team commander, which is all his father would tell him about his SEAL days. "The details are classified," he had said. "The only thing you need to know is that if Alonzo's men find us, I'm more than capable of dealing with them. End of subject."

As soon as the house was secured, and Mack and Christine were enrolled in school, his father had to go to work. The Witness Security Program is not a free ride. Neil was expected to make a living, just like everyone else. In fact, that was part of the cover. Nothing would arouse suspicion quicker than to have a family move into a neighborhood, with parents that had no visible means of support. Another reason the marshals wanted people to work was that people with jobs were less likely to get into trouble, or to dwell on what had happened to them in the past.

His father's options for a regular job were limited. He tried to talk the marshals into giving him his pilot's license back so he could give flying lessons at the local airfield. "Too much of a flight risk," Don told him. (Which is the only joke Mack ever heard him crack.)

With the trial coming up, Mack's father could not be tied down to a regular nine-to-five job, so he decided to try his hand as an independent building contractor. He had always been good at fixing things and knew enough about construction, plumbing, and electrical to get by. The marshals got him a contractor's license, bought him a van and some tools, and *Greene Construction* was born.

Mack's mother wanted to get a job, too, but decided to hold off until after Christine was settled in Los Angeles. Before Alonzo, she had been a real estate agent, and was now considering renewing her license. His father thought it would be great if they could team up. She could buy run-down houses, and he could fix them up to resell or rent out. Mack's mother liked the idea but wouldn't commit to it. Things had gotten better between them since they'd become the Greenes, but their marriage was nowhere near as solid as it had been before Neil's arrest. Their father was clearly guilty of betraying their mother, but both Christine and Mack hoped they'd work it out.

Mack was sitting in the living room thinking about all this, when he heard his father's van pull into the driveway. A moment later, Neil came through the front door, looking a little tired.

Mack was still struck by how much his father had changed since his arrest. He used to have a head of thick black hair, which he kept relatively long. Now it was short, with more gray in it than black. He had never been fat, but he was really thin now, giving him kind of a haunted look. He wasn't out of shape—far from it—he just looked different. When he got out of jail he started running every day,

25

miles and miles, sometimes going out both in the morning and the evening, as if he couldn't get enough of the open space into his system.

But it was more than just his appearance that had changed. His father used to be a big practical joker. He loved a good laugh, even when the joke was on him. Not anymore. Mack guessed that getting caught with an airplane load of dope and worrying about their safety all the time had sucked his sense of humor right out of him.

"Hungry?" his father asked.

"Starving."

"What did you do today?"

"Read a little, worked out."

"When are you going to start running with me?"

Mack gave him a vague shrug. When he was young, he had fallen from his bedroom window, breaking both legs. The doctors said that he might not walk again, and if he did, he would have a bad limp. His father wouldn't accept that. He worked with Mack every day until he was literally back on his feet. No limp, but running was difficult with the steel pins in his legs.

"I'll grab a shower," his father said. "Then we'll head out."

Their favorite restaurant was the Crab Bowl in Kill Devil Hills on the Outer Banks—a resort area on the Atlantic filled with summer homes and hotels.

When they arrived, the restaurant was crowded and the hostess told them it would be at least forty-five minutes before she could seat them. They found a spot outside with a view of the Kill Devil Hills in the distance. This is where Wilbur and Orville Wright had made the first manned flight. Mack asked his father if he missed flying.

He looked at the hills and said, "Every time an airplane flies over."

"Do you think they'll give your license back?"

"Maybe someday. I hope so. But if they don't, it won't be the end of the world. I'm content with what I'm doing now. It's honest work."

He did look content, and Mack was tempted not to ruin his good mood by asking the questions that had been on his mind all day long. But the problem with his father's other moods was that he wouldn't answer questions when he was in them.

"Doris called today," Mack said.

"On the house phone?"

Mack nodded.

His father patted his pocket for the cell, wondering if it had malfunctioned.

"She was calling to check on me," Mack said. "Not you."

His father looked relieved. "What did you talk about?"

"Alonzo's trial."

"She has no business talking with you about that!" He pulled out his cell phone and flipped it open.

"Wait!" Mack said. "It was my fault. I kind of tricked her into talking about it."

His father's eyes narrowed. "Tricked her how?"

Mack told him about the marks on the calendar and how he'd pretended to know more than he did.

His father slipped the phone back into his pocket, then

looked back toward the hills, giving Mack the silent treatment for a couple of minutes. When he turned back, he had calmed some, but Mack could tell he was still irritated. "What did Doris tell you?"

"She said the trial could go on for a long time."

His father nodded. "Alonzo and his attorney are going to fight hard. Everything they have is riding on the outcome."

"Where are we going to stay during the trial?" The trial was being held in Atlanta.

His father looked a little confused, then said, "You're not going to be at the trial."

"What are you talking about?"

"There's no reason for you to be there."

"Are you kidding?" Mack was shocked. "Who else is going to testify about what happened in Elko? I was the one Alonzo came after."

"Those charges have been dropped," he said.

"What?" Mack asked a little too loudly. Several people looked over at them.

"The marshals laid out a pretty good case for letting the whole thing slide," his father said. "They were relieved to have the Elko incident go away. It was embarrassing for them to have the bad guys find someone in the so-called Witness Security Program."

"That was my fault," Mack pointed out.

"We've been over that a dozen times," his father said. "Alonzo already knew you were in Elko. That's why we have to continue to be careful. He may be locked up, but I guarantee he has people looking for us."

Mack didn't say anything for a few moments, trying to digest what he'd just been told. He was looking forward to testifying against Alonzo. But what disappointed him even more was the fact that he wasn't going to see Cat. He thought she would be at the trial to testify and hoped he might get a chance to talk to her.

"What about Sam Sebesta?" he asked. "He certainly isn't afraid of Alonzo."

"You're right about that," his father said. "I don't think he's afraid of anyone."

It was Mack's turn to be confused. His father was talking as if he knew Sam, but he'd been in jail when they were in Elko. "How would you know?"

"He came to see me in jail," his father answered.

"To give you the diary?"

"Not exactly. The day before I got out, they brought me down to the interview room. Sam was waiting for me there. I thought he was another cop. It seemed like every day someone new would show up to ask questions. I nearly tipped my chair over backward when he told me that he was the custodian at your school.

"I don't know how he got in there, but they let him in without question . . . by himself . . . which was unusual. They were very careful about who they let in to see me. Everyone, with the exception of Agent Pelton and your friend Sam, were accompanied by guards."

"He was a Russian spy," Mack said. It was the first time he had told anybody this, but his father didn't look at all surprised.

"A former colonel in the KGB," he said. "But there's

29

more to it than that. To get in to see me, with or without a guard, he would have to know some very important people in our government."

He looked at Mack for a moment, then said, "Sam told me what happened in Elko with you and Alonzo. That was pretty hairy."

"I just did what Sam told me to do," Mack said. "He set the trap."

His father grinned. "He said you were a cool customer. Alonzo and his men had guns, but you didn't panic. Not many kids—not many adults—would be able to keep themselves together in a situation like that."

At the time, Mack had been scared out of his wits, but he didn't mention this to his father. If it hadn't been for Sam he probably would have been a blubbering idiot when the guns came out.

"Sam also told me," his father continued, "there were three other families in your school in the Witness Security Program."

"You're kidding me."

He shook his head. "When the marshals find a location that works, they usually put more than one family there."

"My principal didn't even know about me," Mack said. "At least, I don't think she knew. Does Sam work for the U.S. Marshal Service?"

"Not officially, but the marshals asked him to keep an eye on their witnesses. Doesn't make sense, but there it is."

"*Unai*," Mack said. "Sam's nickname. The Basque word for shepherd. Cat's grandfather, Benat, said the kids at school were Sam's flock. He watched over us."

30

"He did a better job than the marshals," his father said.

"So what happened to the diary?" Jack asked.

"Sam put it in a safety deposit box in a bank across the street from the courthouse where the trial's being held. He gave me one key and kept the other for himself. Did you read the diary?"

"Some of it," Mack admitted sheepishly. His father had told him not to read it. "Just enough to know what it was."

"That's okay. I was going to turn it over to Pelton as soon as I knew you were safe, but you know what happened."

"Alonzo found us."

"Yep, they didn't keep you safe. Sam suggested I hold off on handing it over for the time being. He said it's the only real weapon I have against Alonzo, and I shouldn't give it up until absolutely necessary. So far, I've been able to hang on to it. I'll see how it goes at the trial. If I have to, I'll walk across the street to the bank and make a withdrawal."

"I want to be at the trial," Mack said. "Even if I don't get to testify."

His father shook his head. "Mom and I have already decided. You're not going. The trial could last weeks, maybe months. We'll be stuck in a hotel room under heavy guard. You wouldn't even be able to go out for a walk. For the first time in eight months, Alonzo and his people will know exactly where we are. We'll be vulnerable. Exposed. We are not going to put you or Christine in that situation. It's bad enough that Mom will be there. End of subject."

In their family "end of subject" means "end of subject." This, accompanied by the glare he was giving Mack, made it crystal clear that he was not going to change his mind.

"Where am I going to be while you and Mom are in Atlanta?"

"You'll be in L.A., with Christine."

"For how long?"

"For the duration. If the trial goes into the fall, there's a chance you may have to start school out there. But we'll get you back to Manteo as soon as we can. I'm sorry about all this, but we don't have a choice. There's no place else for you to go."

Mack could think of a lot of other places he would rather be than in Los Angeles with Christine; but his father was right, there really weren't any other options.

"You'll have your own room there," his father continued. "And there's a health club right down the street, where you can work out."

"Did Christine know about this before she left?" Mack asked. His mother was always telling his sister things that she didn't tell him, at least that was his impression.

"Mom didn't drop it on her until this morning."

"How'd she take it?" His sister and he had this love/hate thing going and didn't always get along. Mack suspected that she was even less thrilled than he was with the situation.

"I think she's okay with it."

I bet, Mack thought. "When do I go?"

"Mom's flying back tomorrow. When we go up to Norfolk to pick her up, you're catching a flight to the West Coast."

Day Two

TAKE-OFF

5

Christine listened patiently to the long list of things to watch out for, which her mother had repeated at least a dozen times in the past twenty-four hours. They were on their way to the airport to catch her mother's five-thirty A.M. flight to Norfolk.

"You have my cell number and Dad's," her mother was saying. "And we have yours, of course. Please call us at least once a day. I know it's a lot of trouble, but if you don't call we'll be worried sick. We won't be able to answer if we're in the courtroom, but leave a message so we'll know you're okay. . . ."

Christine tuned her out as she drove down the freeway, surprised at how much traffic there was so early on a Saturday morning.

". . . the membership I got at the health club is a family

membership," her mother was saying. "Maybe you and Mack can work out together sometimes."

Christine glanced at her mother. This was a new list item, and not a very well thought-out one. Her little brother would not want to work out with her at the club, ever. And she wouldn't want to work out with him either.

"It wouldn't hurt," her mother said, catching her expression. "Mack's going through a hard time right now."

Mack/Zack/Jack had been going through a hard time his entire life, in Christine's opinion, and it had very little to do with the name changes or the Witness Security Program. He was strange long before any of that happened.

"Unlike you," her mother continued, "he didn't choose to come out here. We forced him into it."

Christine laughed. "His only other choice was to be sequestered in a hotel room with just you and Dad as company. In two days he'd be begging you to let him come out here. He'll be fine. I'll be fine. The only thing you need to worry about is Alonzo Aznar."

Alonzo Aznar. She still got a little shudder of fear at the mention of his name. Unlike her brother and father, Christine had never seen his face. He was just a silky voice, with a black ski mask pulled over his head and a pistol in his hand.

"You're right," her mother said. "I guess I'm just a little nervous. Here's the airport exit."

Christine took the off ramp.

"What's this thing Hannah had to go to last night?" her mother asked.

"A cattle call," Christine answered. "Instead of an agent

arranging an audition, everyone is welcome to try out. If you don't get in line the night before, all the openings might be filled before you get a chance to audition."

"So everyone just sleeps in line?"

"They bring sleeping bags and food and make a party of it."

"What's she auditioning for?"

"A television thing." Christine knew a lot more about the audition than she was saying. In fact, Hannah had wanted Christine to come with her. But Christine wasn't sure she was ready for something like that. No use in worrying her mother over something that probably wouldn't happen anyway.

She pulled the car up to the curb in front of the terminal.

"Do you want to come in?" her mother asked. "I have some time before the flight leaves."

"I think I should get back before the traffic gets any worse."

"I suppose you're right." Her mother got out and Christine followed her around to the trunk and helped her with her suitcase.

"I'll call you," Christine said, giving her mother a hug.

"You have Mack's flight information?"

"Yes, Mom."

"I love you," her mother said with tears in her eyes.

"I love you, too."

Christine watched her disappear through the sliding door, then climbed into her car and pulled away. On the drive back she found herself thinking of her father—something she had been doing a lot of lately. She missed him and hoped the trial would put an end to the terrible guilt he carried for what he had done to them.

Her thoughts were interrupted by her cell phone. She answered it, expecting it to be her mother.

"Where are you?" Hannah asked.

"Driving back from the airport," Christine answered. "How's it going there?"

"We had a blast last night. Pretty wild, not much sleep, and we're starving. We're holding a spot for you, but you have to bring us muffins, juice, two dozen donuts, and coffee—lots and lots of coffee."

"I don't know," Christine said. "I had to wake up at the crack of dawn to take my mom to the airport. I'm pretty tired."

"You're tired? We've been sitting on asphalt since early yesterday. Really, Christine, you need to come. You'll be going to dozens of cattle calls like this." She laughed. "Well, not exactly like this. Nevertheless, it will be a great experience for you. Please come. Pleeease bring food!"

"How far back in line are you?" Christine asked.

"Oh, a hundred people or so. We're going to get in, that's for sure. There are literally miles of people behind us. They handed out numbers yesterday and we managed to get one for you. Hang on." Christine heard some rustling, then Hannah came back on the phone. "It says: 'Christine Greene, number one-twenty-three.' If nothing else, you can put it in your scrapbook."

Christine sighed. When she had been Joanne Osborne, she had a thick scrapbook with newspaper articles, playbills, even a few reviews. It seemed so long ago. Another life. She had started a new scrapbook in Elko as Wanda Granger, but like the first one, she'd had to throw it away when she became Christine Greene. You weren't allowed to take evidence of your past life into your present life.

"I'll come," she said. "But only if the people behind you don't mind my cutting in."

Hannah laughed again. "Who do you think the donuts are for? It's all been arranged. You're set, little sister."

Christine smiled. She'd always wanted a big sister—it looked as though she had gotten her wish. She hung up and glanced down at her clothes. She was wearing jeans. She wished she had thought to put on something dressier before leaving the house. There wasn't time to stop and change now. They would just have to accept her as she was.

It took her over an hour to get the food and drive to the Rose Bowl in Pasadena, where the auditions were being held. After driving around and around she finally found a parking spot, and with her two heavy bags of provisions, she walked over to the line snaking its way back and forth in front of the stadium. People were singing, putting on makeup, dancing, juggling. There was even a man eating fire, which could not have been very good for his voice. It looked like an audition line for a circus, not a television show, and she began to wonder if she was in the right place.

As she neared the front of the line, she started to see sleeping bags, air mattresses, and camp stoves from those who had spent the night. Some of the people were still asleep, or at least trying to sleep amid the riotous noise and bright morning sun.

"One-twenty-three!" Hannah waved. "Our savior!" She

handed Christine her number in exchange for the two bags, both of which were happily emptied in less than a minute.

A girl came down the line carrying a clipboard, asking for people's paperwork. "Last call!" she shouted. "If it's not filled out and signed, you're not getting in."

"What paperwork?" Christine asked Hannah.

"Oh." Hannah rummaged through her backpack and handed a manila envelope to her with #123 printed neatly on the outside. "It's just a standard release form saying they're not responsible for anything that happens to you, they have the right to videotape you, use your image . . . blah, blah, blah . . . same old stuff."

Christine took the thick sheath of paper out of the envelope and started reading it.

"Last call!" the girl shouted again.

"Hurry," Hannah said, flipping to the last page. "Just fill in the blanks. Name, address, birth date, phone, who to call in case of emergency. . . ."

Christine started scribbling the information down. When she finished, the clipboard girl took it and told her she would have to show a picture identification when she was let through the gate.

A little bewildered, Christine turned to Hannah. "How is this going to work?"

"I don't know exactly," Hannah answered. "But I talked to some people who have been through it before. They said there are a series of auditions in front of different panels of producers. They either pass you up to the next level or you get sent home. If you make the cut tonight, you get a chance to go to the semifinals. Then only twelve people from the semifinals make it to the TV show."

"How long do you think it will take? I have to pick my brother up tonight."

Hannah laughed. "I wouldn't worry about it. We'll probably both be eliminated before lunch."

6

Mack was having a difficult time deciding what to take and what to leave.

He was also nervous about staying with Christine. He was sure the only thing that had kept her going through the rough spots over the past year was the fact that she knew she would be leaving her problems behind when she moved away. His coming to Los Angeles was going to bring it all back, and he didn't know how she was going to react. Christine had two moods—extremely happy or severely upset—with virtually no mood in between.

His father came in to check on his packing progress and found Mack sitting on his suitcase, trying to get it closed.

"Rule of thumb," he said. "If you have to sit on the bag to get it closed, it weighs over fifty pounds."

"I think it's okay," Mack said.

"We'll see."

His father left the room and came back a moment later with the bathroom scale. The suitcase weighed fifty-nine pounds, which meant Mack would have to sacrifice several more items that he really wanted to take.

About halfway to Norfolk, his father's cell phone rang. He repeated the random words and then cut the connection, but kept the phone in his hand, knowing there would be another call.

"The computer doesn't like me to be more than fifty miles away from home base. In about ten minutes, Don or Doris will call to find out what I'm up to."

It took six minutes, and it was Doris. His father listened for a moment, then explained what he was doing and where he was going.

"We shouldn't be up there more than a couple hours. Mack's flight leaves right after Melanie's gets in." He listened some more. "Okay, I'll tell him."

His father disconnected. "Doris says hello."

Mack's flight was delayed by half an hour and his mother's was a little early. To kill time they went into the airport restaurant, where she started to tell them about the house, Christine's roommate, the health club . . .

Her report was interrupted with a voice from their past.

"Neil? Neil Osborne?"

The three of them nearly fell out of their chairs as Chuck Smith, or "Smitty," an old friend of the Osborne family, wove his way through the tables, with a big smile on his face.

"Good lord!" Smitty said. "I thought you'd been abducted by aliens."

Mack's father was the first to get to his feet. He shook Smitty's hand, trying to hide his shock behind something that looked like a smile. Mack's mother was up next. Smitty threw his arms around her, lifting her off the ground. Mack stayed in his chair, but this did not stop Smitty. He came around behind him, grabbed his shoulders, and gave him a bone-crunching squeeze.

"This can't be Jacko?" he said. "The last time I saw you, you were in the hospital with two busted legs. The accident doesn't seem to have stunted your growth any."

Jacko. The nickname brought a smile to Mack's lips. He hadn't heard it in over a year.

Smitty was a cargo pilot for Federal Express, and before that, he and his father were in the Navy together. But Mack wondered if there was more to it than that. Smitty had always been very fit, and still looked strong. Had he been a SEAL like his father?

Smitty pulled a chair up and sat down. "I've been trying get a hold of you on and off for about a year. I called your house. The phone was disconnected. I called your cargo out-fit. Same thing. What gives?"

"We moved," his father said.

"Obviously." Smitty laughed. "Where to?"

"Kansas City."

"What about the cargo business?"

His father shrugged. "Couldn't make a go of it. Not enough business for us little guys."

"Tell me about it," Smitty said. "Us big guys aren't faring much better. To tell you the truth, I'm getting a little fed up flying boxes around, myself. It's kind of a letdown

44

from what we used to do for living. What are you doing in Kansas City?"

"A little of everything. Pilot training, consulting, flying left seat for the rich."

Mack had to hand it to his father. He sounded pretty convincing. His mother, on the other hand, was still stunned, sitting mutely with a frozen smile pasted on her face.

"What brings you to Norfolk?" Smitty asked.

"Vacation," his father answered. "Some friends of ours have a beach place at Hilton Head."

His father's cell phone rang and he pulled it from his belt like it was a six-shooter, put it to his ear, then realized his mistake. The computer was giving him the series of words that he couldn't possibly repeat in front of Smitty.

"Excuse me," he said, and walked away from the table.

Smitty gave him a curious look, then turned to Mack's mother. "Going or coming?"

"What?" his mother said, obviously startled.

Smitty pointed at Mack's backpack and his mother's carry-on. "Are you headed down to Hilton Head or flying back to K.C.?"

His mother just looked at him. She didn't know what to say.

Mack came to her rescue. "Neither," he said.

His mother shot him a look. He didn't care; if she kept faltering, Smitty was going to know something was up.

"We've been here a week," Mack continued. "But I have to cut it short. I'm going to Los Angeles. A friend of mine

45

and his family are meeting me and we're driving down to Disneyland."

"Sounds like fun," Smitty said.

Mack's father came back to the table, but didn't sit down.

His mother got up. "I guess we'd better get you on that flight, Jack. You don't want to miss Mickey."

Mack's father gave her a confused look.

"Hey," Smitty said. "There's an Osborne missing. Where's Joanne?"

"Kansas City," Mack's mother answered, getting into the spirit of the deception. "Working. Trying to earn some extra money for college."

"College?" Smitty said. "Wow. Time flies."

There was an awkward silence, and by the look on Smitty's face it was pretty clear he hadn't completely bought their story. "You sure everything's okay?"

"Couldn't be better," his father said.

Smitty locked his gray eyes on him for a moment, then glanced at his watch. "Well, I guess I better be pushing off too." He pulled a business card out of his wallet and gave it to Mack's father. "Jot your number down. I get out to K.C. once in a while." He handed a second card to Mack's mother. "In case you forgot how to get ahold of me."

Mack watched his father write a number down that probably didn't even have the right area code.

"I'll give you a call," Smitty said, then gave each of them a final bear hug.

As they watched him walk away, his father said, "That did not go well."

46

"Disneyland?" his mother said, looking at Mack.

"It's all I could think of on such short notice."

"What are you two talking about?"

"I'll tell you on the drive home," she answered. "If Mack doesn't hurry he's going to miss his flight, and he still has to go through security."

"That's right," his father said. "The leg pins."

Mack nodded. If he were to go through the metal detector stark naked, the alarm would still go off, which really slowed things down.

"Do you have your cell phone?" his mother asked.

"Yeah."

"Call us when you get to your connecting gate in Chicago."

"Okay."

"And try to get along with Christine. She's looking forward to having you out there."

I bet, Mack thought, stepping into the security line.

"You're in!" Hannah shouted, jumping up and down. "I can't believe it!"

Neither could Christine. Throughout the long, grueling day, the contestants had been whittled down one by one until there was hardly anyone left in the stadium. Hannah had made it through three rounds. A friend of hers had made it through the fourth round. Each time Christine auditioned, she thought it would be her last. More than nine thousand people had tried out, and it was now down to forty-two contestants. This was no longer a lark; she actually had a chance to make the semifinals, and perhaps even be picked as one of the final twelve.

A producer had just announced that the forty-two contestants were being bussed to a hotel in Beverly Hills for the semifinals.

"I know you're all tired and hungry," the producer said.

"But you've made it this far, so hang tough. We'll feed you when we get to the hotel and you might even be able to get a catnap in, because it's going to take a while to get everyone through."

"What about our cars?" someone asked.

"We'll provide a shuttle back to the stadium," she answered. "Or, if you have a friend here, they can drive your vehicle over to the hotel."

"How long will this take?"

"That depends on where you are on the list, which I'll pass out in a minute. All the auditions will be wrapped up tonight, however long it takes."

She passed the list out to moans and cheers. Christine eagerly ran her finger down the list and was crestfallen to see that she would be the thirty-fifth person to step into the room with the final judges.

"You're going all the way, little sister," Hannah said. "I just know it."

"I don't even know if I'm going to get on the bus," Christine said.

"Are you crazy? I'd crawl on my stomach through broken glass to get to that hotel."

"I won't be done until midnight, maybe later. I have to pick up Mack."

"Don't even think about it," Hannah protested. "I'll pick him up and bring him over to the hotel."

"I don't know," Christine said.

Hannah put her hands on Christine's shoulders and looked into her eyes. "You need to get a hold of yourself. I know you're tired and nervous, but this is the opportunity of a lifetime. Don't even think about passing it up."

Christine took a deep breath. "I guess you're right."

"I *know* I'm right." Hannah held her hand out. "Give me your car keys."

Day Three

FAME

8

Because of his late departure from Norfolk, Mack nearly missed his connection in Chicago.

As he made his way down the narrow aisle of the airplane, his cell phone rang. He fished it out of his backpack as he climbed over two rather large people and wedged himself into the window seat.

"Did you make your connection?" his mother asked.

"Barely," Mack said. "It's about to take off."

"I've been trying to reach Christine, but she doesn't answer."

"She knows when I get in," he said. "She'll be there." One thing about his sister was that she was punctual. Too punctual, in Mack's opinion. She had made him look bad his entire life.

"It isn't like her not to call," his mother said.

"She's probably cleaning the house and can't hear her phone." That was the other thing about his sister Mack didn't like. She was an absolute neat freak. He looked over and saw a flight attendant standing in the aisle, glaring at him. "The door has been closed," he informed Mack. "All cell phones must be turned off for the duration of the flight."

Mack nodded and told his mother he had to go.

"Call me as soon as you land."

"It'll be three in the morning your time."

"I don't care."

"Okay, but I really have to go. Bye."

The flight attendant continued to glare until the phone was off and stowed away.

Mack was asleep before the jet reached cruising altitude, and he didn't wake up until the landing gear touched down at LAX.

He expected Christine to be waiting for him in the baggage claim area, but she wasn't there. He kept his eye out for her as he watched the baggage carousel. One by one, people grabbed their bags until there were only about a half dozen passengers left, wondering if they were going to have to stomp over to the lost baggage office. But they were in luck. A final load of luggage appeared on the belt. Among them was Mack's fifty-pounder.

Now, he thought, if they only had a lost sister office, I'd be in good shape.

He dug his cell phone out and gave her a call. No answer. He was beginning to think his mother might have good reason to worry. Christine was never late for anything. And if she was going to be late, she would call, or at least have her cell phone on so he could call her.

54

"Mack?"

Startled, he turned around. A very cute girl was hurrying toward him.

"Welcome to L.A.," she said. "Sorry I'm late. I'm Hannah."

Before he could respond, she had her arms around him. She planted a kiss on his cheek, which was nice but a little embarrassing. He looked past her shoulder, expecting to see Christine sauntering up, but he didn't see her.

"Where's Christine?"

"At an audition."

Mack looked at his watch. "At twelve-thirty at night?"

"It's been a long day," Hannah said with a disarming smile. "I'll explain everything in the car. You're a lot better looking than Christine let on."

Mack was really embarrassed now and felt himself turning red. To hide it, he looked down at his phone and started to dial.

"Christine has her phone off," Hannah said.

"I know . . . uh . . . I need to call my mom and tell her I got here okay."

"It's three-thirty in the morning on the East Coast," Hannah said. "I'm sure she's asleep."

Mack shook his head. Hannah did not know his mom very well. She'd be wide awake, waiting for the phone to ring.

"You can't tell her Christine wasn't here to pick you up," Hannah said.

Mack looked up. "That's going to be a little hard. She's going to ask to speak to Christine. If I don't call her, she'll call 9-1-1 and put out an all points bulletin for me."

Hannah laughed. "I see your point. You'd better let me talk to her."

He finished punching in the number and gave Hannah the phone.

"Hi, Melanie? This is Hannah. . . . No, everything's perfect. His plane was a little late and he's getting his bag. He wanted me to give you a call so you could get to bed. . . . Oh, I know. Her phone wasn't charged, and we didn't discover it until we were leaving the house. She's in the car, waiting for us to come out. It's a lot easier than parking in the lot. . . . I'll tell her to give you a call tomorrow morning as soon as she gets up. . . . All right . . . You, too. Go to bed. We're all fine."

Hannah flipped the phone closed and handed it back. By Mack's count, she had told seven lies in less than twenty seconds. She would fit right into the Witness Security Program.

"What was that all about?" he asked.

"Christine doesn't want your mother to know about the audition until it's all over. It's kind of a surprise."

Mack wondered if she had just told her eighth lie.

"Is that your only bag?"

"That and my backpack."

"Well, grab them and let's get out of here."

"To your house?"

Hannah shook her head. "Beverly Hills first," she said. "Then home."

9

Christine tried to get a nap in, but it was impossible with all the noise and video cameras filming everything they did. There had been cameras at the stadium, too. But spread out among nine thousand contestants, they weren't nearly as inhibiting.

They had been divided into small groups based on their position on the list and put into holding rooms to wait their turn. A producer poked his head through the doorway and said that he thought Christine's group would be moved up to the audition floor in ten or fifteen minutes.

"How many people have made it through to the semi-finals?" a contestant asked.

"One," the producer said.

"You're kidding?"

"Nope. The bar's been raised this year. In some cities, we haven't even picked a single person."

At least this will be over soon, Christine thought wearily. She glanced at the clock on the wall. Hannah should have picked up Mack by now. She knew she should call to make sure, but she wanted to stay focused. There was no point in going through all this, only to get distracted at the last moment.

She went into the restroom to get away from the cameras and to decide which song she was going to sing. For the previous six auditions she had performed the same song, or at least a small portion of it, but this time she was thinking about changing her tune. The collective wisdom of her group, many of them who had been through this before, was to stick with the same song that got you here. Christine wasn't convinced.

During her brief life in Elko as Wanda Granger, she had tried out for the high school musical, *The Opera Ghost*. The songs had all been composed by Sam Sebesta, that odd custodian from Mack's old school. The signature piece was beautiful and showed off the full range of her voice. Ever since they'd arrived at the hotel, it had been playing in her head, almost as if it were calling to her.

Someone knocked on the door and said the producer was back. Christine came out.

"They're ready upstairs," the producer was saying. "You won't be coming back here, so take all your things with you. If you're eliminated, you'll be escorted down to the lobby, where your friends and family are waiting."

There were ten people in her group. They squeezed into the elevator and rode up to the top floor. With the cameras following their every move, they were ushered into a small lounge, where they were told to sit down and relax. Sitting was not a problem. Relaxing was impossible.

After about ten minutes, a security person came through a set of double doors and called the first person inside. Within five minutes, he was back out, with a stricken expression on his face. All he said to them before being escorted to the elevator was, "That was brutal!"

The next person was in and out in less time than the first. "They are in a very bad mood," she warned.

The third, a girl who Christine thought was really talented and very funny, was inside for over ten minutes. They expected her to come out all smiles, waving her ticket to the semifinals. Instead, she came out in tears, too upset to even speak.

Christine started to get mad. She had seen the judges on television and knew how cruel they could be. She could just imagine what they were saying to the contestants, most of whom had been up for well over twenty-four hours, waiting for this one chance. She was determined not to let the judges get under her skin. She was not going to come back through the door crying—no matter what the outcome.

Number thirty-four was called inside. Christine was next. She closed her eyes and sang her song in silence, hitting all the notes perfectly in her mind. She had sung the song hundreds of times, but not in front of a real audience. They'd had to leave Elko before the first *Opera Ghost* rehearsal. When they moved to Manteo, she took the lead character's name.

"Christine Greene?"

Christine opened her eyes in surprise. She hadn't even seen number thirty-four come back out.

"What happened?" she asked.

"Close, but no cigar," thirty-six answered.

"Follow me," a producer said.

Christine took a deep breath to calm herself. A security guard held the door open, and they stepped through.

The three familiar judges were sitting behind a table, looking much smaller than they did on television. On the left was Bo Winston, wearing a huge gold watch. On the right was Angus Killick in a tight red T-shirt. And between them was the tiny Madge Cardillo. All of them looked exhausted and distracted, as if they wanted to be anywhere but there. The room was filled with bright lights and cameras. Makeup people were busily working on the three judges. When they finished, Madge looked over at Christine and gave her a smile.

"How are you, Christine?"

"Good," Christine said. "A little nervous, but happy to be in here."

"Waiting is the hardest part," she said, glancing down at the sheet of paper in front of her. "So, you're a new L.A. transplant. Where'd you move from?"

"Manteo, North Carolina."

"Hmm. We've had some great singers from North Carolina. What are you going to sing for us tonight?"

Bo glanced at his big watch. "This morning," he corrected.

Angus closed his eyes and leaned back in his chair, his arms folded across his chest.

"It's from *The Opera Ghost*," Christine answered.

"Never heard of it," Bo said.

"It's never been recorded, as far as I know. It was

60

composed by a man named Sam Sebesta, who I'm certain you haven't heard of either."

"It's a little risky singing an original tune," Bo commented.

"A risk I'm willing to take," Christine said. "The song means a lot to me. It came from another time. Another life."

"Go for it," Bo said.

Christine looked at each judge in turn. Angus was still leaning back in his chair with his eyes closed. She decided that her goal was to get him to lean forward and open his eyes. Even if she didn't make it to the final round, if she accomplished that one thing, she would be happy.

She began to sing. By the fifth note, Angus's eyes opened. By the tenth, his arms came down and he was sitting up straight. He wasn't smiling, but he was paying attention. They let her sing for much longer than she'd expected. Finally, Bo held up his hand for her to stop.

"Wow, dawg, that was good . . . I mean really good. You've got some pipes." He looked over at Madge. "What do you think?"

"Fabulous," she answered. "One of the hardest things to do is to pick the right song for your voice. You took a chance, and it paid off. Nice job."

Christine looked at Angus, who rarely had anything nice to say to anyone. "You don't really need my vote, considering the overblown response from Madge and Bo. But it was okay. Somewhat different from the others who have assaulted our senses today."

Christine wasn't sure if he was giving her a compliment or insulting her.

"How old are you?" he asked

"Eighteen."

Angus looked a little surprised. "What's even more interesting to me than your voice," he said, "is your underlying toughness."

Christine was a little taken aback by the comment. She didn't think of herself as particularly tough. No one had ever called her that.

"I'm serious," he said. "There's something there. And in this business, being tough is just as important as the sound of your voice."

She didn't know how to respond, so she just stared at them, waiting for their decision.

Angus looked at Madge and Bo. "Well?"

"Definitely," Bo said.

Madge smiled. "Congratulations, Christine."

Angus looked back at her. "You never know," he said. "You might just be the next American SuperStar."

10

Hannah bought Mack a hamburger on the way to the hotel and gave him a step-by-step rundown of Christine's day. She told him that when she left the hotel, only one performer out of nine thousand had made it through.

Mack didn't expect to be spending his first night in L.A. waiting to hear if his sister would be a semifinalist on American SuperStar.

He watched the show every week with his family. They all loved music, and it was fun arguing about who they thought was the best singer. It was one of the few times during the week they functioned like a normal family, without the shadow of Alonzo hanging over them.

His mom and dad were always saying that Christine's voice was better than any of the finalists. Christine always brushed their remarks off as ridiculous.

But apparently, she had taken their comments more seriously than Mack thought. He was genuinely excited for his sister and understood why she wanted to keep it a secret from their mother and father for the time being. There was no use getting them all worked up unless she made the semifinals. They worried more about Christine's high school play auditions than she did. Something this major would have driven them up the wall.

Mack liked Hannah. Mostly because she didn't treat him like a little kid. By the time they got to the hotel he began to think that spending a few weeks in L.A. wouldn't be so bad after all.

A policeman stood outside the hotel and checked their names against a list before letting them in. The hotel lobby was crowded with dozens of people waiting for their friends or relatives to come down from the audition room. No one seemed to know what was going on upstairs. As a result, when the lobby elevator opened, they didn't know who would step out.

Some of the singers came out crying, some smiling, but none of them had made it all the way. The rumor was that the judges were fed up with everything and were running through the remaining people as quickly as they could so they could go home and go to sleep. Mack thought there might be some truth to this, because the elevator seemed to be spitting contestants out into the lobby almost as fast as it could get up to the top and back down.

A little after two in the morning, the elevator made three relatively quick trips. Then there was a long delay of at least a half an hour. This got everyone's attention. Finally, the elevator started down again. The crowd watched eagerly as the floor numbers above the door counted down.

"Something's up," Hannah said, pointing to three cameramen rushing over to the elevator.

She and Mack followed them. Halfway there, the doors slid open, and Christine stepped out with a huge smile. Hannah rushed past the cameras and grabbed her.

"Well?"

"I made it to the semifinals!" Christine said.

The girls jumped and screamed amid loud cheering and clapping from the crowd. Then Christine spotted Mack. She broke away from Hannah and gave him a hug.

"Sorry I wasn't at the airport," she said.

"No problem. *American SuperStar*, huh? Wow."

"I still can't believe it!" Christine grabbed Hannah's hand. "Let's get out of here. I'm starving."

"I know a great diner in Hollywood," Hannah said.

It took them nearly twenty minutes to get through the swarm of people congratulating and peppering Christine with questions about the remaining contestants still upstairs. When they finally got to the car she asked Hannah to drive, saying she was too hyper to be trusted behind the wheel.

The food at the diner was as good as Hannah had promised. And they weren't the only ones sitting in a red leatherette booth eating breakfast at three in the morning. The place was jammed with a bizarre assortment of people. Hannah and Christine barely gave any of them a glance in their excitement over the audition. Mack, on the other hand, almost forgot his food, he was so interested in the crowd.

"Even if you don't get into the final twelve," Hannah was saying, "you'll still be able to sign up with any talent agency in town. They'll all want you in their stable. You're going to get a lot of exposure."

The last word snapped Mack's attention back to the conversation. *Exposure.* Hannah was absolutely right.

Mack looked at Christine. She was grinning from ear to ear. The meaning of what Hannah was saying had obviously missed her completely. The Greenes could not afford exposure. They were supposed to lay low, live a quiet life. Being a contestant on *American SuperStar* is not what the U.S. Marshals had in mind for people in the Witness Security Program. Don and Doris were going to implode when they found out.

His mother and father had encouraged Christine to try to make a go of it as an actress and singer, but what they had in mind for her was four years at UCLA, by which time Alonzo would have hopefully forgotten all about them. In their wildest dreams, they didn't anticipate Christine getting a shot at fame within twenty-four hours of her mother leaving her in Los Angeles.

Mack wanted to blurt the problem out right then, but couldn't. Hannah had no idea who they really were. He tried to recall what the cameras caught when Christine stepped out of the elevator. Everything, he thought. Including Christine giving me a hug. All of Christine's friends watched *American SuperStar*, including the friends she'd had when she was Joanne Osborne and Wanda Granger. They were going to wonder why she was calling herself Christine Greene now. It would be the talk of her old high schools, and spread like wildfire through the small towns where they used to live.

"When's the semifinal round?" he asked.

"Next month," Christine said.

This made Mack feel a little bit better, but not much. By then Alonzo's trial might be over and there would be no point in him trying to hurt them. At least, that's how Mack hoped it would go.

"Oh, my God!" Christine shouted.

"What?" Hannah asked.

Mack thought Christine had finally caught on.

"School," she said. "It starts September twenty-seventh. If I'm lucky enough to make it into the top twelve I'll miss the whole term."

Mack clamped his mouth shut.

Missing some school was going to be the least of her problems, he thought. And mine.

11

Alonzo was up early, as usual. He sat on the cot in his tiny cell, reading his e-mail, while the television droned on in the background.

His e-mail contained nothing new, nothing that would help him. If he were on the street, he would know by now who the Osbornes had become.

His younger brother, Raphael, reported that some of Alonzo's men were looking for other opportunities, making inquiries with his competitors. Alonzo shook his head. Betrayal like this would be punished. He began tapping out a reply to Raphael, telling him exactly what to say to the traitors at the annual cartel meeting, or "jamboree," as Raphael called it.

The jamboree was being held in three days on the Aznar vineyard in South America. People from all over the world flew in for it—some new recruits, some longtime members of the cartel. In many cases it was Alonzo's only opportunity to talk face to face and tell them what he required of them in the upcoming year. But this year, for the first time, Alonzo would not be able to attend. Raphael would have to pass the information on to the members himself. And this had Alonzo worried.

Raphael was a good brother, but impulsive and a little eccentric. Alonzo constantly had to rein him in, which was difficult from a jail cell.

When Alonzo had been arrested, Raphael wanted to break him out. He had devised a detailed plan, assembled a group of professionals, and was in the process of putting the plan into action when Alonzo finally got wind of it. It took several heated e-mails to get Raphael to stand down and call off his men. Alonzo did not want to be on the run for the rest of his life; he wanted to be acquitted. His business depended on his being able to travel freely in the United States. Bender had already managed to get many of the charges dropped. A prison escape was a last resort—one that Alonzo would certainly consider—but only when the time was right.

He was halfway through Raphael's e-mail when an urgent e-mail came in from a trusted source telling him to watch *Entertainment AM*, a popular morning television show. Alonzo switched the channel, not knowing how this was going to help him, and got back to his e-mail to Raphael.

A few minutes later, his work was interrupted by the sound of a familiar song. He looked up just in time to see the smiling host of the idiotic morning show come back on.

"When we return from our break we'll see who got lucky yesterday in Pasadena in the SuperStar race, and who went home. . . ."

Alonzo turned the volume up and waited impatiently through the toilet paper, car, antidepressant, and dish soap commercials. Someone shouted for the volume to be turned down. Alonzo ignored him. The host finally came back on. . . .

"More than nine thousand young hopefuls showed up at the Rose Bowl in Pasadena, California, yesterday, and only two— that's right, two—were good enough, in the judges opinion, to move into the next round. . . . "

A man wearing a red T-shirt came on. The interviewer asked him about the poor showing in L.A.

"The bar's been raised," the man said with an arrogant shrug. *"Los Angeles is only one of a half dozen cities we'll be visiting. Two out of nine thousand is better than zero out of nine thousand. . . ."*

The camera cut to a young man singing in front of three judges. When they told him that he had made it to the semifinal round he jumped up in the air with a shout and punched the air with his fist.

"And the other lucky singer is a girl named, Christine Greene."

Alonzo leaned toward the screen, tempted to jump up and punch the air himself. She was no longer blond and blue-eyed, but there was no mistaking the voice, or the song, which he had last heard in Elko, Nevada.

"So, you're a new L.A. transplant," the pretty judge said. *"Where did you move from?"*
"Manteo, North Carolina."

The camera followed the jubilant Christine Greene down to the lobby, where she was met by a girl with red hair and a boy. Alonzo had never seen the redhead before, but he knew the boy.

He also knew a lot of people in Los Angeles. Some of his best customers were there.

He started tapping out a series of e-mails. He would have to move swiftly before the Greenes and the marshals realized their mistake.

12

Mack didn't wake up until after eleven.

He needed to catch Christine away from Hannah so he could talk to her about the problem, but she wasn't up yet, and neither was Hannah. He knew better than to wake her. His sister wasn't at her best when she first rolled out of bed.

He found cereal and milk in the kitchen and toured the house while he ate. It was a nice place, but he wondered how long they would be around to enjoy it. Out back was the lemon tree his mother had talked about. He had never seen one before, and was about to go out for a closer look, when Christine's cell phone rang. Normally he wouldn't even think about answering it, but the phone was sitting on the kitchen table and he saw on the caller identification that it was his mother.

She was obviously relieved to hear his voice. "I got worried when you didn't call," she said.

"We're fine," he told her. "We kind of had a late night."

"What were you doing?"

He wasn't about to tell her what they were really doing. He would leave that up to his sister.

"Taking in the sights," he said.

"Isn't the house great?"

"Yeah, it's nice. I'm looking at the lemon tree through the back window."

"Is Christine there?"

"She's still asleep."

"Asleep?"

"I told you, we were up late."

"How late?

"I don't know . . . late. I slept on the airplane so I wasn't tired. Christine and Hannah weren't either."

"Isn't Hannah a doll?"

"Yeah."

His mother sighed. "I guess I should let you go. You're all set up at the club. When you go out the front door, take a right. It's about three blocks up the street. You can't miss it. But if you go before Christine gets up, leave her a note so she knows where you are. And have her call me."

"I'll tell her."

Mack took his mother's suggestion and walked down to the club. It was packed with very fit, attractive people, who looked like they spent a lot more time working out than he did. He was a little self-conscious among the bronze gods and goddesses, but the equipment was much better than the stuff they had at home.

73

When he got back to the house, Christine and Hannah were up, and as excited as they had been the night before. But their frenzy had nothing to do with *American SuperStar*. It was Hannah's turn.

"My agent called!" Hannah screeched when he walked through the front door. "She never calls. I always have to call her. Anyway, a famous director, Vincent Smooth—he did the films, *Oh, My Dog!* and *The Sound of One Hand Clapping* . . . Have you see them?"

Mack shook his head. He had never even heard of them.

"Well, he's been hired to make a Pepsi commercial for the Super Bowl and he wants me to play one of the leads."

Mack didn't know that commercials had lead roles.

"It's an unbelievable break for me," Hannah continued. "Apparently, he saw one of my screen tests, then looked at my portfolio, and said this is the girl I want. No audition, not even an interview. I've got the part. Done deal. The planets must be perfectly aligned over our house. The next thing we know, *you're* going to get a gig."

I already have a gig, Mack thought. I'm playing Mack Greene.

"Anyway, I have to fly to Vancouver," Hannah went on. "The commercial's being shot in Canada. Cheaper to film there. I'll be back in two or three days. Four at the most, my agent says." She looked at Christine. "Come help me pack."

Christine started to follow her into the bedroom. Mack grabbed her by the sleeve. "Uh . . . Mom called."

"You didn't tell her, did you?"

"No, I thought I'd leave that for you."

"She's going to be so excited."

"She sure is." But not in the way you think, he thought.

"I'll call her as soon as we get back from the airport. I have to drop Hannah off. Do you want to come?"

"I guess."

Four hours later, on the way back from the airport, Mack was finally alone with his sister.

"I think you might have slipped up," he said.

She glanced over. "What are you talking about?"

"The SuperStar thing. It might have been a huge mistake."

"Mistake?"

"Exposure," Mack said. "All the cameras. Someone from our old life is going to recognize you."

Driving down the freeway at seventy miles an hour was probably not the smartest time to bring it up. Christine swerved and sideswiped the car in the next lane.

When she got the car back under control, she pulled onto the shoulder, then broke down sobbing, her head on the steering wheel. The man they hit was pretty nice about the whole thing, considering he had spilled hot coffee all over his three-piece suit and the trim had been ripped off the side of his brand new Mercedes. He thought Christine's breakdown was a result of the accident, and tried to comfort her as they exchanged license and insurance information.

It was early evening by the time they started out again. Mack didn't say another word about slipping up, and neither did Christine, until they pulled into the driveway of the bungalow.

She turned the engine off and said, "I can't believe I was so stupid!"

"Join the club," Mack said. He knew exactly how she felt, having done something equally stupid the year before in Elko.

"I got so caught up in the moment, I didn't even stop to think about what it all meant."

"It may not be as bad as you think," Mack said. "I mean, they may not even use the footage of you coming out of the elevator."

"That's not the only footage," Christine said. "There were cameras around me all day long. So many that I forgot they were even there most of the time. You've seen the show. They love those candid moments. I signed a release that I didn't even read. I'm sure it gives them the right to air anything they want."

"The question is, *when* are they going to show it?" Mack said. "If it's not too late, Doris and Don can ask the network not to air any of it."

"Maybe. But however you look at it, I'm still out of the semifinals. It's over." She started crying again.

"Not necessarily," he said. "There's a chance that Alonzo will be convicted by the time the show starts."

Christine grabbed his hands. "Do you think so, Jack?"

She hadn't called him by his real name in a year. "Sure, *Joanne*," he said.

"Oops," she said with a laugh. "Another slipup."

Mack smiled. "I talked to Doris a couple days ago. She thinks it's in the bag. Alonzo's going away for a long time."

"I hope you're right. I really want this. I mean . . . I'm not saying I'm good enough to get into the final twelve. But if I do, I'll have a shot at winning."

"I think you could go all the way," Mack said, and he meant it. "We're not cut out for the witness security thing. We keep screwing up. If you win, you can hire personal bodyguards for all of us."

"It's a deal!" she said, then let out a long sigh. "I guess we should go in so I can call Mom and Dad."

The first thing Mack was going to do when he got inside was hit the kitchen and eat. He hadn't had anything since the bowl of cereal, and he was starving.

13

A man grabbed Mack as soon as he stepped through the door. He gave the man a head butt in the nose and drove him back into the wall.

"Run, Christine!"

But it was too late, and there were too many of them. Another man ran up and slugged Mack in the stomach. He doubled over, gasping for breath. His arms were jerked behind him, and his wrists were cinched tight with plastic manacles.

The man Mack smashed in the nose stood above him, blood all over his shirt, his fists clenched like two stones. Mack thought he was going to kill him right there, but another man with a crew cut walked up and pushed him away.

"I'll give him to you later if he causes any more problems," Crew Cut said. He looked at Mack. "Tough guy, huh?"

Mack was still struggling to breathe. He didn't feel very tough. His forehead hurt from butting the guy, and he thought he was going to puke. Crew Cut hauled him to his feet and half carried, half dragged him to the sofa, where his sister was sitting, crying.

It took Mack a couple of minutes, doubled over, to get his breath back. When he looked up, he saw four men. Two of them were holding pistols.

"Who are you?" he asked.

"Delivery men," Crew Cut answered. He was obviously the ring leader.

When Alonzo had come into their house a year ago, he and his men were wearing ski masks, so they couldn't be identified. These men hadn't bothered to disguise themselves at all. Mack was more worried about that than he was about the guns.

"What are you delivering?" he asked.

"The Greene children," the leader said. "Formally known as Jack and Joanne Osborne."

The man's cell phone rang. He took it out of his pocket and flipped it open. "We have them. Did the roommate get on the plane? Good."

"Hannah has nothing to do with this!" Joanne said.

"Joanne's right!" Jack added. There was no point in hiding who they really were now.

The man cut the connection. "Relax. She's getting a free trip to British Columbia. She'll be a little disappointed when she gets there, though. No Pepsi commercial. By the time she gets back, you two will be long gone."

"Where are we going?" Jack asked.

"Don't know. My job is to deliver you. And I could care less where you end up, or what happens after I turn you over."

"To who?"

He shrugged. "Look, we're just doing a job here. If you cooperate and don't cause us any more trouble, you'll live. If you bug me, you won't. Your questions are bugging me. So shut up." He turned to his men. "You two go ditch the girl's car. When you get back, park the van in the driveway near the back door."

The man Jack had head-butted was standing in the kitchen doorway, holding a dish towel over his nose. Crew Cut told him to go to Joanne's room and pack her things. "Don't worry about the boy's stuff. He hasn't had time to unpack. Just bring his suitcase and backpack."

He dumped Joanne's purse out onto the table and picked up her cell phone. "You won't be needing this." He turned it off.

"My parents are going to call," Joanne said. "If I don't answer they'll be worried."

Crew Cut smiled. "I suspect that's exactly what we want them to do." He looked at Jack. "All right, sport, stand up. I'm going to pat you down."

All he found was Jack's wallet, which he put on the table. He searched Joanne next. She had some loose bills in her pocket, a pack of gum, and a tube of lipstick. He scooped their things into a plastic bag. The other man came back out carrying their suitcases.

"Okay," Crew Cut said, "just a couple more things to take care of here and we'll be on our way. I assume your parents have an e-mail address?"

80

Jack and Joanne didn't say anything.

"I'll take that as a yes." He pulled a small digital camera out of his pocket and took their photo, then tossed the camera to the other man.

"I'll need that e-mail address now."

"I don't know it," Joanne said.

"That's too bad." He pulled a knife out of his pocket and flipped it open. "Luckily, we have your home address in Manteo. I guess we'll just have to send a couple of fingers or an ear to your folks to prove that we have you." He yanked Joanne to her feet and held the knife to her throat and glared at Jack. "Which part of your sister do you want me to put in overnight mail?"

Jack blurted out the e-mail address.

"I thought that might jog your memory." He nodded to Bloody Nose. "Use the roommate's computer to send the photo."

Bloody Nose went into Hannah's room.

"One more thing we need to do," Crew Cut said. He sliced Joanne's manacles and shoved her back down onto the sofa. "I need you to leave a note for your roommate." He put a sheet of paper and a pen on the table in front of her. "Something about how there was a family emergency and you and your brother had to fly home. And you'd better make it convincing. We don't want her getting suspicious and calling the cops." He gave them an unpleasant smile. "In fact, all of your lives depend on the cops staying out of this. We'll be keeping an eye on Hannah. As you said, she's not involved. Let's keep it that way."

Joanne started writing.

Bloody Nose came back in. "The picture is on its way."

"Good."

Joanne finished the note and pushed it across the table.

Crew Cut read it over. "That ought to work. Tie her back up and put the hoods on."

Bloody Nose tied her wrists, then slipped a black cloth bag over her head.

Jack was next.

Everything went black.

14

Alonzo spent the entire day in his cell, monitoring his e-mail.

It was a complicated plan, put together hastily, with many people involved. A lot could go wrong. His brother, Raphael, was overseeing everything, but El Sereno and Zita Vega, two of his most trusted lieutenants, were coordinating the operation in the U.S.

Typical of Raphael, when he heard that they knew where the Osbornes were, he wanted to fly to L.A. and take the children himself. It took several e-mails, but Alonzo finally convinced him to stay where he was, arguing that they could not afford that kind of risk. *If I lose you, Raphael, all is lost*, he had written to him. *You are the only thing holding our business together. And there is the jamboree to consider. What happens there is vital to our future. Let Zita and El Sereno take the risk. They are expendable.*

Zita and El Sereno were not expendable, but the little lie had worked on Raphael. Reluctantly, his brother had agreed to stay where he was.

Alonzo loved Raphael, but he was much better suited for their business south of the border. He had spent very little time in the U.S. and did not appreciate the delicacy in which things must be handled here. Two years earlier, Raphael had lost his temper in a restaurant in Houston and had gotten into a gun battle. There was a warrant out for his arrest. If they caught him in the U.S., he would be put in jail immediately, and it was unlikely that he would ever get out.

Another e-mail came onto his small screen. It was from El Sereno. The message simply read: *We have them.*

Alonzo opened the attached photo and smiled at the frightened Osborne children sitting on the sofa. And now, he thought, I have Neil Osborne.

He replied to the e-mail with one word: *Proceed.*

15

"Why doesn't she answer?" Melanie asked as she paced their living room. "Why doesn't she call? This isn't like Christine. Something's happened."

Robert was worried, too. Melanie had called Christine a dozen times in the past couple hours.

"We'll give it another twenty minutes," he said. "Then I'll call Doris. They'll send people from their L.A. office over to the house to check on them."

"I should have stayed there until Mack was settled in," Melanie said, and started crying.

Robert tried to put his arms around her, but she shook her head and stepped way.

The phone rang. Melanie lunged for it and saw Christine's name on the caller I.D.

"Christine?"

"No, Mrs. Osborne, this is not Christine," a man with an odd accent said. "And Christine is not your daughter's real name, *Patricia*. Put Neil on the line."

Patricia stared at Neil with wide, frightened eyes. "Pick up the extension."

Neil ran into the kitchen and came back out with the cordless phone pressed to his ear so hard that it hurt.

"Are you on the line, Neil?"

"Yes." He sat down on the edge of the sofa.

"Do you know who this is?"

"El Sereno," Neil said quietly. The Watcher. Alonzo's eyes and ears. "Where are Joanne and Jack?"

"Safe," El Sereno said. "For the moment. Whether they stay that way rests solely in your hands."

Patricia let out an anguished sob.

Neil felt the same despair, but fought to control it. "How do we know they're safe?"

"Check your e-mail."

Patricia rushed over to the computer and turned it on. Neil joined her. It took a few frustrating moments for it to boot up and retrieve the e-mail. She opened it. No message, just a photo. Joanne and Jack sitting next to each other, looking terrified.

"Do you see them?" El Sereno asked.

"Is that blood on Jack's face?" Patricia shrieked.

"Yes," El Sereno said mildly. "And there'll be more if you don't do as we say."

"I want to talk to them," Neil said.

"No."

"Then we'll call the police."

"Call them," El Sereno said. "And you will never see your children again."

"Alonzo's not going to get away with this."

"He already has. And trust me, none of this can be traced back to him. He has the perfect alibi. He's in jail. Or have you forgotten?"

"I haven't forgotten," Neil said. "What do you want me to do?"

"There are three conditions for their release," El Sereno said. "First, you will give us information about the prosecutor's case so our attorneys can prepare their defense. Second, you will change your testimony, but not until the very last moment. Not until you are on the stand, and not until we tell you. This is critical. You and Patricia must not tip our hand. We do not want the prosecutors or the police to know anything about the change beforehand. For this to work, it must come as a complete surprise."

"You want me to lie on the stand," Neil said.

"Of course," El Sereno said. "You will take the blame for everything, which is what you should have done in the first place to avoid all this unpleasantness."

"What's the third condition?" Neil asked.

"The third condition is the infamous diary you have been keeping. We must have it. I trust you haven't given it to the police?"

"I have it," Neil said.

"Where?"

"In a very safe place."

"Don't play games with me, Neil."

"I'm not," Neil insisted. "I can't get it right now, and

neither can you. I'll say anything you want at the trial. When it's over—and the children are safe—I'll give you the diary, but not before."

This was followed by a long silence. Then, El Sereno spoke, "I will discuss this with Alonzo. But understand. The next time I ask where the diary is, you will tell me, or one of your children will die."

Neil did not respond, but inside he was screaming, *Please don't hurt my children!*

"Tomorrow morning," El Sereno continued, "you will receive a package. In it will be a small handheld computer. There will be no more phone calls. We will communicate with you through e-mail. You will need to take the computer with you when you and Patricia are sequestered for the trial. The computer is wireless and completely secure. When you open an e-mail you will have exactly ten minutes before the message, any attachment, and the reply address are permanently destroyed. Are you looking at the photo of your children?"

"Yes."

"In the lower right-hand corner is a stamp with the date and time. To keep you motivated, we will send you a new photo once or twice a day. Watch."

The digital image of Joanne and Jack disappeared from their screen.

"If you betray us again, Neil, you will not like the next photo we send. Do we have an agreement?"

"I'll do whatever you want," Neil said.

"Please don't harm the children," Patricia pleaded. "They had nothing to do with this."

"I hope that won't be necessary," El Sereno said. "Do you have any other questions?"

"How did you find us?" Patricia asked.

"You mean you don't know?" El Sereno gave a dry, humorless laugh. "Your daughter was on national television this morning. She was auditioning for that *American SuperStar* show that is so popular here."

Patricia closed her eyes.

Day Four

THE BUNKER

16

Jack and Joanne were shoved into the back of a van.

After two or three hours, the van stopped and they were let out into what Jack assumed from the echoing sound and the smell of fuel, was a huge airplane hangar.

Jack heard Crew Cut ask about his money. There was a zipping noise like a duffle bag being opened then closed. Crew Cut said it was nice doing business with them, then the van started and drove away.

Someone slapped Jack on the head and said, "No talking!" which he thought was unfair because he hadn't said a word.

Next he was led up a set of steep stairs, prodded down an aisle, pushed into a seat, and belted in.

At first he thought he and Joanne had been separated, but as the engines started, she called out for him. She was somewhere behind him. Jack shouted back that he was there, which earned him another slap on the head. Knowing she was close by was worth it. He guessed that Joanne got a slap, too, because she didn't say anything after that.

The jet took off.

Jack was tired, mad, and hungry. His seat belt was too tight and his hands were numb. But mostly, he was scared. Every once in a while he could hear Joanne whimper.

To prevent himself from becoming totally unhinged he concentrated on putting their situation into some kind of perspective. Except for the punch to the stomach and the two slaps to the head, he and Joanne had not been hurt. This was good. The fact that the men had taken their photograph and sent it to their parents meant that they wanted something from them. No doubt something to do with Alonzo's trial.

He didn't think his parents would tell the marshals they'd been kidnapped. And even if they did, he didn't think the marshals would be able find them. With a hood on he couldn't tell for sure how long they had been flying, but it was at least five or six hours, with one brief refueling stop.

However long it had been, it was long enough to be out of the United States if they were flying south. Long enough for Jack to really have to use the lavatory.

"Hey!" he shouted. "I gotta pee!"

It took about five seconds for the head-slap.

"You can hit me all you like," he said. "But that's not going to solve the problem. I'll go right here if that's what you want."

He braced himself for another slap, but it didn't come.

Instead, he felt the buckle unsnap, which was a huge relief just by itself. He was yanked to his feet, turned, then marched down the aisle. His escort shoved him into a closet-size room and slammed the door behind him. Unfortunately, this didn't relieve the situation.

"At the risk of getting hit in the head again," he yelled, "this is not going to work."

The door opened. He heard loud, truculent breathing. For a horrible moment he thought it was Bloody Nose.

"Sorry," Jack said, in a more reasonable voice. "I can't see what I'm doing. And with my hands tied behind my back, I can't do what I need to do."

More breathing, an exasperated grunt, then a click. His hands were freed. Next, the hood was snatched from his head, along with a clump of his hair. He blinked in the bright light, turned to get a look at his captor, and stumbled backward in shock. It was a woman holding a switchblade. She was very tall, with short, spiked red hair, skintight jeans, a black tank top, and biceps bigger than his.

"You got a problem?"

It was the same voice that had told him not to talk back in the hangar. Her voice was deeper than Jack's.

"No," he stammered. "I just . . . uh . . . no . . . no problem."

She glared at him with the most unusual eyes he had ever seen. The irises were golden with almond-shaped pupils, like a snake's. Jack would not have been surprised if she hissed at him.

"Do your business and be quick about it." She slammed the door.

It took about three minutes for enough feeling to come back into his hands to do his business. When he finished, he took a look at himself in the mirror and wished he hadn't. There was a large goose egg on his forehead and dried blood from the man with the nose bleed all over his face. He washed, then gulped down several little paper cups of water from the stainless steel washbasin.

Snake Eyes was waiting for him outside the door. He expected her to retie his hands and pull the hood back over his head. Instead, she pushed him back down the aisle a few seats past Joanne and pointed. He sat down, and, before he knew what was happening, she had a handcuff snapped around his right wrist and the armrest.

"If you open your mouth," she warned, "the hood goes back on."

He really wanted to ask her who she was and where they were going, but he kept his mouth shut. Snake Eyes did not strike him as the type to give someone a second chance.

She walked back to where Joanne was sitting. "Okay. Your turn."

When Joanne returned, Snake Eyes made her sit down in the seat across the aisle from Jack. She handcuffed her to the armrest, snapped their photograph, then stepped behind the front bulkhead, presumably to e-mail the image to their parents.

"I'm sorry," Joanne said quietly.

Jack put his finger to his lips and shook his head. He did not want that hood back on. He glanced at his watch, then looked out the window. The sun was rising on the left side of the jet. Stretching beneath them was an endless sea of blue, which had to be the Pacific. The coastline was too far away to see anything clearly, but they had to be flying along the west coast of Central, or South America.

Snake Eyes came back down the aisle without so much as a glance in their direction. Jack craned his neck around and saw her disappear into the lavatory.

"You have nothing to be sorry about," he whispered.

Joanne didn't hear him. She had put her seat back and was sound asleep.

17

Neil and Patricia spent the entire night trying to figure out what to do. By sunrise, they still hadn't reached a decision.

Physically exhausted and emotionally spent, Patricia got up from the sofa. "I can't think anymore. I'm going to try to get some sleep."

"Good idea," Neil said. "There's nothing we can do until the package gets here anyway."

Neil was tired, too, but knew he would not be able to sleep. He put on his running gear and stepped outside into the humid morning. His usual route was down to the Manteo harbor and back. But today he headed west, past the site of the Lost Colony, and over the bridge to the Alligator River National Wildlife Refuge. Running calmed him and helped him to think more clearly. The other reason for the run was security. This is why he chose to run over to the refuge rather than the harbor. The labyrinth of dirt roads crisscrossing the refuge were seldom traveled. If Alonzo's people or the authorities were watching or following him, Neil could spot them out there.

The most obvious solution to the problem was to do what they asked—give them the diary, feed information from the prosecution's case to Alonzo's attorney, then, at the last moment, change his testimony. Neil would go to prison, which he was more than willing to do if it meant Joanne and Jack would be freed, unharmed. But there was no guarantee that Alonzo would fulfill his part of the bargain.

Neil looked at his watch, surprised to see he had been running for nearly an hour. He hadn't seen a single car since he'd gotten to the refuge. To make sure he wasn't being followed, he jogged over to a tree he had spotted the last time he'd come this way. In the upper branches was a camouflaged stand for hunting deer. He climbed up to it and scanned the roads, thinking about what he should do.

Their second option was to tell the marshals what had happened. Patricia and he had discussed this at great length, but it was not really a consideration anymore. Jack and Joanne were no longer in the country, Neil was certain of that. It would take the various law enforcement agencies weeks to organize a rescue. By then it would be too late.

There was a third option, which he had not discussed with Patricia because it was too crazy, too risky. But it might be their only chance.

Neil got back to the house just as a delivery truck was pulling up to the curb. He took the small package from the driver and went inside, surprised to see Patricia up. She was sitting at the kitchen table drinking a cup of coffee.

He handed her the package.

There was no message on the small handheld, just a photo. Jack looked a little better than he had in the previous photo, although there was an ugly bruise on his forehead. Joanne was disheveled, but appeared unharmed.

"They're on a jet," Neil said, pointing to the tiny screen. "You can see the rows of seats in the background." He hesitated, then said, "I'm not going to change my testimony. I'm not going to do what Alonzo wants."

Patricia gave him a resigned nod, as if she had expected this.

"I'm not going to tell the marshals the kids have been kidnapped either," he continued. "They'd never be able to pull off a rescue in time."

"You're right," Patricia said quietly.

This was not the reaction Neil had expected, but he pushed on anyway.

"I have to get out of here before Doris and Don find out about Joanne's television debut. As soon as they do, they're going to round us up and put us someplace safe. I can't help the kids if I'm locked up in some hotel."

"You're going after Joanne and Jack," she said.

"Yes."

"That's what Sam thought you would do," Patricia said.

"Sam Sebesta?" Neil asked in shock.

"He called right after you left."

"How did he get our phone number?"

"I didn't ask," Patricia said. "He heard about Joanne. He

wants us to fly to Elko to meet him. If we leave for the airport now, we can be there this evening."

"Why?" Neil asked. Flying to Elko, Nevada, was definitely not part of his plan to rescue the children.

"Sam wants to help us," Patricia answered. "You can't do this alone, Neil."

"How's Sam going to help?"

"First, he's going to try to stop the marshals from coming after us. He thinks Alonzo has sources inside the Marshal Service. As soon as they find out we're gone, Alonzo will know we went after the kids."

"We?" Neil asked. "You're not coming with me."

"They're my kids, too," Patricia said.

"It's too dangerous, Pat. You have no idea what these guys are capable of."

"I'm going," Patricia said. "End of subject." She walked into the bedroom and came back carrying two bags. "Let's go get our kids."

Neil couldn't help but smile. Patricia was a step ahead of him, as usual. And she was going with him, whether he liked it or not. End of subject.

The cell phone rang. He answered and repeated the words the computer gave him for the very last time, then disconnected.

"We won't need this anymore," he said, setting the cell phone on the kitchen table. "Time to go."

"There's a plane to Salt Lake City that leaves in four hours," Patricia said. "From there, we can catch a commuter flight to Elko. Somewhere along the way, I need to dye my hair. Sam said—"

"Wait a second," Neil interrupted. "I have some ideas about how to go about this myself. The first thing we're going to do is steal a jet. I know a very paranoid dope dealer who has a dozen secret hangars across the U.S. and Latin America, just in case he needs a fast getaway. The closest one is a short cab ride from the Dallas/Fort Worth airport."

"Then what?"

"I guess we fly to Elko to see Sam." And he hoped he could talk her and Sam into staying there. It was a good place for Patricia to hide out until this was all over. "Now, what's this about dying your hair?"

"Sam's idea," Patricia answered. "No one in Elko knows what you look like, but everyone there knows me. He thought it would be a good idea if I changed my appearance." She glanced in the mirror. "I've been thinking of changing the color anyway. What would you think of a raven-haired beauty with very short hair?"

"I'd love her no matter how long or what color her hair was," Neil said. "Let's go."

18

Joanne slept during most of the flight, which was just as well. Jack was sure that whatever she was dreaming about was better than thinking about the situation they were in. Snake Eyes, their flight attendant from hell, didn't sleep at all. She was coiled up five rows back, reading a trashy supermarket rag.

When Jack was a kid he used to play this game called *Where in the World Is Dad?* He had a map of the world in his bedroom with routes laid out in different colored yarns. His father would call and ask: "Where am I, Jacko?" With a watch and an airline schedule Jack was usually able to figure out exactly where he was. He was playing a new game now called *Where in the World Are Jack and Joanne?*

He knew that Alonzo was from Bogotá, but he didn't think that's where they were going. By his rough navigation they had passed Colombia several hours ago.

The jet banked sharply to the east toward the Andes mountains, waking Joanne. She blinked a few times, then let out a moan of dismay when she remembered where she was. Jack tried to give her a reassuring smile, but it didn't have the effect he wanted. She started crying silently.

Jack could not stand to see his sister cry—or anyone else, for that matter. He looked out his window, concentrating on the magnificent mountains stretching north and south as far as he could see.

On the other side of the mountains, the jet started an ear-popping descent, leveling out over a hilly agricultural area. Jack tried to figure out where they were. No rain forest canopy, which meant they weren't over Ecuador or Peru. That left Argentina.

They passed over a town. He tried to remember the names of the cities in Argentina. The only one he could think of was Buenos Aires, but the town below was too small and too far west.

The jet descended into a wide green valley, then flew over a huge lake with a paved runway along the shore. The landing gear snapped into place, and a few moments later they came in for a landing and taxied to a stop.

As Snake Eyes unlocked their cuffs, Jack thought about slugging her and running for the hatch. But where would he go once he got outside? And there was Joanne to consider. He couldn't very well leave her behind.

As if she could read his mind, Snake Eyes locked her golden gaze on him and said, "Don't try anything. We don't need to keep both of you alive. In fact, it would be easier if one of you were dead." She re-cuffed them together, left to right wrist, then shoved them down the aisle to the exit.

The jet was parked at the end of the runway. A van with the back doors open was waiting for them at the bottom of the steps. Snake Eyes tossed their suitcases into it as if they were empty. Jack looked toward the hangar at the opposite end of the runway. Above it was a large sign.

Before he had a chance to look around further, Snake Eyes pushed them into the windowless van, slamming the doors behind them. As they drove away they heard the jet engines restart.

"Where do you think we are?" Joanne asked.

"Aznar Vineyards," Jack said. "In Mendoza, Argentina."

"As in South America?"

"Unless they moved the country, yeah."

"This isn't funny, Jack. How do you know?"

"I read the sign above the hangar."

"Alonzo has a vineyard?"

"Apparently."

"Who's that woman?"

"Snake Eyes? I have no idea, but she's plenty scary."

"I think she's wearing contacts," Joanne said.

"Why would someone make their eyes look like that?"

"For effect."

"Creepy."

About five minutes later the van slowed and came to a stop. When Snake Eyes opened the back door she was talking to someone in Spanish on a two-way radio.

She signed off, clipped the radio to her belt, then said in English, "Bring your suitcases."

Handcuffed like they were, getting the bags out was easier said than done. Carrying the bags was going to be even harder.

The van was parked near what looked and smelled like a horse barn. Snake Eyes pointed to a small door. "In there."

"What is this?" Joanne asked.

"No talking!"

The van drove away as they half dragged, half carried their suitcases through the door. Inside were thirty stalls, fifteen on each side, most of which were empty. Aside from Snake Eyes there wasn't another human in sight. She stopped them in front of a stall with a black stallion in it. Jack wanted to suggest they might be more comfortable in an empty stall, but held his tongue.

The sign above the stall said: DIABLO. Jack didn't know much Spanish, but he knew enough to know the name meant *Devil*.

"Stay clear," Snake Eyes said, grabbing a halter hanging on a hook near the stall. "He only likes Raphael."

Who's Raphael? Jack thought, but he didn't dare ask.

"He also hates children," Snake Eyes said.

He didn't seem to like Snake Eyes much either. They stepped back and watched as she tried to slip the halter on. Diablo danced around the stall, kicking and biting. Jack cheered him on silently, hoping he would stomp her to death, but it was no contest. Snake Eyes was as quick as a rattler and had the halter buckled on in less than a minute.

She led Diablo past them and cross-tied him in the walkway. "Pick up your bags and get into the stall."

"You've got to be kidding me," Joanne said.

Snake Eyes was clearly surprised at the outburst. Jack wasn't. The reason he'd never gotten a dog as a kid was because of Joanne's dislike of animals and the messes they left around. She really had a phobia about it. A single mouse dropping would send her up a wall, literally, with surgical gloves and a bucket of disinfectant. The stall was actually pretty clean, with only one pile over in the corner. But that was one too many piles for Joanne.

"Get in the stall," Snake Eyes repeated, snatching a riding crop off the wall.

"We better do what she says," Jack said.

Joanne shook her head. "I've had enough of this."

So had Jack, but he didn't think this was the place to make a stand. Snake Eyes was moving toward them with the crop raised.

"You'd be surprised what one of these will do to your face," Snake Eyes said.

This was about the only thing she could have said to change his sister's mind.

Jack did not like the sly smile Snake Eyes gave them when Joanne jerked him into the stall. She was not smiling because Joanne had obeyed. She was smiling because she had just discovered two of Joanne's biggest fears: filth and defacement. Snake Eyes knew how to control her now.

It turned out that Joanne had given her the information for nothing, because they were just passing through. A hidden door slid open in the back of the stall. Beyond the door was a stairway.

Snake Eyes unlocked the cuffs, then pushed them through the passageway.

107

Jack and Joanne bumped their suitcases down the steep stairs. At the bottom was a short cement hallway with a single door at the end, which Jack was certain concealed an elaborate torture chamber.

Snake Eyes reached into her pocket and took out a ring with several keys on it. She found the one she was looking for, opened the door, and then pushed Jack and Joanne inside. The door slammed and they heard the key turn. They were locked in.

It was not a torture chamber. Far from it. There was a living room with a sofa and a couple of comfortable-looking chairs, shelves full of books, DVDs, videos, a big-screen television, a stereo system, a good-sized kitchen stocked with ample food, two bedrooms with king-sized beds, a fully stocked bar, a utility room with a washer and dryer, and a large bathroom, which Jack used immediately.

When he came back out, Joanne was looking at the DVDs and videos.

"They're all old Westerns," she said.

Jack went over and looked at the books. All of these were Westerns, too. In fact, the whole place had a western motif, including the leather sofas and chairs, which were covered with the cow hair still on the hide.

"I guess it isn't so bad, as far as prisons go," Joanne continued. "How long do you think they'll keep us here?"

Jack shrugged.

"What do you think Mom and Dad will do?" Joanne asked.

Again, Jack shrugged.

"I don't understand what they want from us."

"What they've always wanted," Jack said. "They want Dad to back down. And they're using us to make him do it."

"Will he?"

"Sure," he answered, with a lot more confidence than he felt.

"Then they'll let us go?" Joanne asked.

Jack hoped the answer would be yes, but he had serious doubts. The apartment had a permanent feel to it, as though they had just been buried alive. What worried him even more was that, except for Snake Eyes, they hadn't seen anyone since they got there. The pilots hadn't opened the cockpit door, they hadn't seen the van's driver, and there were no grooms in the barn. Nobody knew they were here. The grave was unmarked.

"What are you thinking?" Joanne asked.

Jack wasn't quite ready to share his concerns with his sister yet. "I'm thinking about how hungry and tired I am," he said.

Joanne heated up a couple of cans of stew, which Jack gulped down like a hungry wolf. After he finished, he stumbled into a bedroom, flopped down on the bed, and was asleep as soon as his head hit the pillow.

Six hours later, he was rudely awakened by the lights snapping on and a slap on the face. Snake Eyes jerked him to his feet by his hair and had his arm twisted behind his back before his bleary eyes could focus.

"You don't need to—"

"Shut up!" She tightened the pressure on his arm and

hair, and marched him into the living room in his under-wear.

Before this demonstration, Jack was still playing with the idea of trying to overpower her. That didn't seem like a good idea anymore. If he didn't kill her with the first punch, she'd tear him apart.

She pushed him onto the sofa next to Joanne and snapped their photo. "I'll be back in twelve hours to take another photo. You'd better be ready."

They watched her stomp through the open doorway, then slam the door closed.

"Are you all right?" Joanne asked.

"I guess." Jack hurried into the bedroom and came back out with his pants on. "You might have given me some warning."

"I would have if she had given *me* some warning," Joanne said. "She came bursting through the door, told me to stay where I was, and a second later, came out of the bedroom with you in hand. This place must be soundproof. I didn't hear a thing until she came through the door."

"Soundproof, huh?"

Joanne nodded, then her eyes narrowed in suspicion. "What are you thinking?"

"Do you think that two-way radio she carries works down here?"

"I doubt it. Why?"

"I don't know," Jack answered vaguely. "Maybe we should start thinking about how to get out of here."

"And go where?" Joanne asked, obviously not thrilled with the idea.

"Mendoza," Jack said. "We can find someone there to help us."

Joanne shook her head. "It's too risky. And like I said earlier, this place isn't so bad. They haven't really hurt us."

"Yet," Jack said, rubbing his sore arm.

19

Neil and Patricia hurried through the Dallas/Fort Worth terminal and caught a cab to a nearby private airfield.

"What if the jet isn't there?" Patricia asked quietly, so the cab driver couldn't hear.

"There'll at least be a small airplane and a helicopter. All the hangars are set up the same way. Alonzo likes options. He always has an exit strategy in case he gets in trouble. If the jet's not there, I'll fly the small plane to the next hangar. One of them is bound to have what we need."

"How many pilots does Alonzo have?"

"Now that he's grounded, I don't know," Neil answered. "When I was flying for him, he had ten pilots on twenty-four-hour call, and three full-time mechanics who flew in and out to take care of the birds."

The cab pulled up to a large hangar at the end of the runway. Neil paid him, then led Patricia to a small door in the back. He punched in the combination on the keypad, pushed the door open, and flipped on the light. Inside was a small twin-engine airplane, a helicopter, and a sleek Learjet.

"Why weren't these confiscated when they arrested him?" Patricia asked. When Neil was arrested, the DEA had taken everything the Osbornes owned, including their house and cars.

"They don't know he has them," Neil said.

"I thought you told—"

"I didn't tell them everything," Neil interrupted. "And I'm glad I didn't. I'll give them the rest after we get Jack and Joanne back."

"The diary," Patricia said.

"Yep, it's all in there. But I'm not turning it over until we're all safe."

"Do you think that will ever happen, Neil?"

"I hope so." He pointed to a door in back of the hangar. "There's a restroom and shower through there. While you're doing your makeover, I'll pre-flight the jet and calculate our route."

When Patricia came out, she no longer looked like Melanie Greene, Mary Granger, or Patricia Osborne.

"Wow," Neil said.

"Should I take that as a compliment?"

"Definitely. A big one. They're not going to recognize you in Elko."

20

U. S. Marshal Doris Welty had had a terrible afternoon, and it looked as though it was going to be an even worse evening.

It started right after lunch, with a phone call from a reporter. He was from the Osbornes' former town and wanted to know why Joanne Osborne had changed her name to Christine Greene. Doris spent over an hour trying to convince him not to run the story he was working on. He finally gave in when she told him that if he did print the story, he would be directly responsible for any harm that came to the Greene family as a result of him revealing their true identity.

She got a copy of Joanne's audition tape and called a grumbling Don Smites in from his vacation. They watched the tape in stunned silence.

"What was she thinking?" Don yelled.

"She was thinking she has a fabulous voice," Doris said.

"And a chance of being the next American SuperStar. It was a huge mistake, but she's only eighteen."

This did little to calm down her partner. "The Greenes are history," he said. "We'll have to move them, change their names, start all over again."

"The Greenes may already be gone," Doris said.

"Now what are you talking about?"

"Robert's missed the last three calls from the computer."

"Where's his cell?"

"At the house, according to the tracking signal. But no one's answering the house phone, either."

Don cursed.

"I sent a local cop to the house about an hour ago," Doris said. "He said no one came to the door, but there were lights on in the house, and Robert's van was in the driveway."

Don sat down and put his face in his hands.

"I'm afraid there's worse news," Doris said.

Don looked up. "What?"

"I called the house in L.A. where the kids are staying and talked to Christine's roommate, Hannah. Told her I was a producer from *American SuperStar*. It turns out that Hannah was sent on a wild goose chase to Vancouver, B.C., last night. She was supposed to have had some part in a commercial or something up there. Anyway, it was all bogus—no crew, no camera people, no director. She spent the night in the airport, sleeping in a chair. When she got back this afternoon, there was a note from Christine saying she and Mack had to leave for some kind of family emergency."

"Maybe the emergency is that Christine realized she slipped up," Don suggested.

115

"Or maybe Alonzo saw the same thing we just saw," Doris said. "And had his people kidnap them."

"If that's the case," Don said. "Alonzo moved pretty fast." He started pacing. "We'd better put someone on the roommate, in case Alonzo sends someone back there to clean up loose ends."

"I already talked to the L.A. office," Doris said. "They're staking out the house."

"Has anyone grilled Alonzo about this?"

Doris shook her head. "I spoke to Agent Pelton over at Drug Enforcement, and to the prosecutors at Justice. They want to keep a lid on it for the time being. If this isn't Alonzo's work, and the Osbornes have decided they've had enough and took off on their own, the prosecutors don't want Alonzo and his crooked lawyer to know their star witness has flown the coop."

"Makes sense," Don said. "What's our next move?"

"We need to fly down to Manteo, get inside the house, and see if we can figure out what happened."

"It could be as simple as the kids got spooked, flew home, and the Greenes are on their way to the airport to pick them up," Don said hopefully. "In their haste, Robert might have left the phone in the house."

Doris looked at him doubtfully. "Either way," she said. "If they're in Manteo, we still need to get down there and talk to them and figure out what we're going to do about this mess."

21

Patricia and Neil landed in Elko a little after six P.M. and took a cab to the Nevada Hotel, where Sam Sebesta rented a room. They went up to the third floor and knocked on his door. No one answered.

"He's probably downstairs eating with the other boarders," Patricia said.

Neil looked at his watch. "I guess we'll have to wait. I don't want to approach him in front of a bunch of people."

"We might as well eat, too," Patricia said. "I don't know about you, but I'm hungry."

"I could eat," Neil said.

The restaurant on the first floor of the hotel was crowded as usual, and the Osbornes were told it would be ten or fifteen minutes before a table would be available. They waited in the adjacent bar, which was also packed. Patricia recognized a few of the people, but none of them seemed to recognize her. They'd only been in Elko a few months before Alonzo found them, but she was sure the Grangers were the talk about town for several weeks after they left.

The hotel and restaurant were owned and operated by Catalin Cristobal's parents.

"That's Catalin," Patricia whispered, pointing to a young girl with long black hair carrying a platter of sizzling meat into the restaurant.

"She's beautiful," Neil said. "I can see why Jack is having a hard time getting over her."

A sad look crossed Patricia's face. "I think that's the worst thing about this whole situation. Jack and Joanne can't go after their dreams and desires like other kids. The simplest decisions have to be scrutinized and rescrutinized for potential risk to the family and others. It's not fair."

"It's worse than that. It's impossible," Neil said. "At least for this family. As soon as we get them back—and we will get them back—we're going to become the Osbornes again."

"How?"

"I don't know, exactly. But I'm not going to have you and the kids looking over your shoulders for the rest of your lives because of my mistakes. One way or another, this is going to stop."

Patricia was about to ask him to clarify what he meant, when Catalin's mother walked up and told them that their table was ready.

Sam was sitting at the head of the boarders' table in the dining room. Sitting next to him was Smitty. Neil did a double take, then looked at Patricia.

"I called him," she whispered, nudging Neil toward their table.

He took his seat and glanced over at Smitty and Sam, who didn't appear to notice them.

"Who else did you call?" he asked quietly.

"Just Smitty," Patricia answered. "He was about to fly a load to upstate New York when I caught up with him. I guess he canceled that flight and came down here instead."

Neil would not have brought Smitty into this mess, but he was glad to see him. Smitty was not only the best SEAL operative he had ever worked with, he was also the best pilot he had ever seen, and qualified to fly the stolen Learjet parked at the Elko Regional Airport.

"What did Smitty say when you told him?" Neil asked.

"You mean after he stopped swearing?"

"Yeah."

"He said he was relieved to hear we were in the Witness Security Program. He thought we didn't like him anymore."

Neil grinned.

Catalin was their server. When she came to the table she gave Patricia a curious look as she explained the menu. Patricia avoided making eye contact and let Neil give their order so Catalin wouldn't recognize her voice.

"I think she knows who I am," Patricia said after Catalin walked away.

"She might," Neil said. "But I think we're okay."

Midway through their meal, Sam and Smitty got up and left the restaurant. Ten minutes later the Osbornes paid their bill, went back up to the third floor, and knocked on Sam's door.

"Come in."

Smitty came over and gave both of them a bear hug. "We'll get 'em back," he said.

"Thanks for coming," Neil said.

"I ought to kick your—" Smitty glanced sheepishly at Patricia. "Well, you should have called me sooner."

Sam motioned for them to sit. Patricia realized that the room was virtually empty, except for a duffel bag and an aluminum briefcase sitting on the floor. The last time she had been in this room, it was littered with stacks of books, magazines, and CDs. Now there wasn't even a bedspread on the mattress.

"Did you move to another room, Sam?" she asked.

"Actually, I moved to another country," Sam answered. "But we'll talk about that later. Right now I want to hear about what happened."

As Neil talked, Patricia could not help but notice the change in Sam. He was no longer the gentle, easygoing custodian from Elko Middle School. There was a hard edge to him she hadn't seen before.

When Neil finished, Sam sat in the chair, with his head down for a long time without saying anything. Finally, he looked up. "Tell me more about this El Sereno."

"The Watcher," Neil said. "Alonzo uses him to keep an eye on things for him. He's an expert on surveillance. I suspect he's the one that came up with this handheld computer gimmick."

"How old is he?"

"I only met him once. I'd guess he's your age. Maybe a little older."

"Is he South American?"

"I don't think so. He's has an accent. Eastern European. Why is El Sereno so important?"

A small smiled played on Sam's lips. "I used to know a man who called himself 'The Watcher.' He was very good at what he did. I wondered what had happened to him. But let's get back to the business at hand. I think you're safe from the federal marshals. At least for the time being."

"I don't know how you did it," Neil said. "But thanks."

"Do you know where Jack and Chris—" Sam hesitated. "I don't know your daughter's real name."

"Joanne," Patricia said.

Sam nodded, then looked at Neil and said, "Colombia or Argentina?"

Neil stared at him in surprise. "How—"

Sam held his hand up. "I did a little research about our friend Alonzo Aznar after he put a gun to my head. Just in case he decided to pay me another visit. So, which is it?"

"My guess is Argentina," Neil said. "Alonzo and his brother Raphael have a vineyard and winery outside Mendoza. It's a front for their drug business. We used to fly in there all the time."

"Raphael Aznar," Sam said. "Reportedly worse than his brother. A cowboy nut."

"That's Raphael," Neil agreed. "Dresses and acts the part, six-shooters and all. He's a real piece of work. Learned English watching Westerns. He built a town right out of the Wild West at the vineyard. They call it Durango. He spends most of his time riding his horse around the estate, sleeping outside most nights. He and Alonzo are total opposites.

121

Alonzo never saw a gadget he didn't want. Raphael hates technology or anything modern. He's not nearly as clever as Alonzo, and they won't be expecting anyone to come after the kids—especially me. As far as he and Alonzo are concerned, I'm just an ex-navy fighter jockey. They didn't even know I was fluent in Spanish until after I was arrested. They have no idea what I used to do for a living."

Sam smiled for the first time. "You were a SEAL operator," he said. "You saw action in Beirut, Iraq, Republic of the Congo, Guatemala, and other war-torn places."

"How could you know that?" Neil said. "That's all classified. You couldn't possibly get that information without the highest security clearance."

"Who are you, Sam?" Patricia asked.

It was Sam's turn to be surprised. "Jack didn't tell you?"

Patricia shook her head. "All he said was that you were much more than you appeared to be."

Sam stood up. "We can talk on the airplane."

"Wait a second," Neil said. "By getting the marshals off my back, Sam, you've done enough. There's no reason for you to come along." He turned to Patricia. "And I think it might be better if you stayed here with Sam. Smitty and I can handle—"

"I'm going," Patricia said, standing.

"I'm going, too," Sam said quietly. "I have no doubt that you and Smitty can get the job done, Neil. But what will that accomplish if the Aznars are still after you and your family? I have a plan that will not only get Jack and Joanne back, but, with a little luck, it will make this whole thing go away. The Aznars, your legal problems . . . all the bad things from

122

the past year. I've done this kind of thing before. But, for the plan to work, you need to trust me."

Neil looked at Smitty, who had been uncharacteristically quiet since they came into the room. "What do you think?"

Smitty shrugged. "I've only known Sam for a few hours, but he strikes me as a guy who can be trusted. If his plan comes apart, you and I can always clean up the mess." He looked at Sam and grinned. "We've done that kind of thing before."

Sam returned his grin. "Fair enough." He picked up the aluminum briefcase and opened it on the bed. Inside was a laptop computer and what looked like a cell phone, which he took out. "You're probably familiar with this," he said.

"It's a VX iridium satellite telephone," Smitty said, obviously impressed.

"The last time I checked," Neil added, "the VX was strictly a military piece of hardware."

Sam slipped the phone into his pocket without further explanation. He picked up his duffel bag and briefcase, and they were about to leave, when there was a knock on the door. It was Catalin Cristobal.

"I need to speak to Mrs. Granger," she said.

Sam turned and looked at Patricia. She gave him a resigned shrug, and he let her in.

Patricia gave her a hug. "So, you recognized me."

"Not right away. I actually recognized you," she said, pointing at Neil. "You look so much like Zach . . . or whatever his name is now."

"His real name's Jack," Neil said. "It's good to meet you, Cat. He talks about you a lot."

"Really?" Cat gave him a shy smile. "Is he here?"

"Uh . . . no . . . he . . ."

Patricia came to his rescue. "Jack's with his sister."

"Of course," Cat said. "In Los Angeles. I saw her and Za—I mean, Jack, on TV. I guess things are going well for your family if she could go on TV like that."

"We're still having a few problems," Patricia said. "And I need to you do me a favor."

"Sure, anything."

"I need for you to keep our visit here a secret."

"I won't tell anyone," Cat promised. "And I don't think anyone else in the restaurant recognized you." She pulled something out of her pocket. "Jack sent this to me just after he left Elko." In her hand was a small toy astronaut.

"Commander IF," Neil said quietly. Jack's imaginary childhood friend. When Jack was nine years old and in the hospital with two broken legs, Neil had given his son the toy astronaut. After Jack got out, he carried the figure with him everywhere he went. "I haven't seen this in years. I wondered if Jack still had it."

Cat looked at him for a moment, then said, "I know you aren't telling me everything. You probably can't. But will you give this to Jack for me? He said Commander IF was a good friend when he was a kid. He gave him to me to keep me company. I have a feeling that he might need a friend right now. Tell him it's just a loan. I want Commander IF back."

She handed the toy figure to Neil, then looked at Patricia, with tears in her eyes. "I'd really like to see Jack again, if possible. I miss him."

"He misses you, too." Patricia gave her another hug. "I can't promise, but I'll see what I can do."

124

Doris and Don were inside the Greenes' house. They found the cell phone on the kitchen table and evidence of hasty packing in the master bedroom. There was no sign of a break-in or struggle, which was a relief to both of them.

"They didn't pack enough for a long trip," Doris said. "My guess is that they're planning on coming back here."

"Yeah," Don said. "But where did they go? And why?"

"I'll put a bulletin out on their car," Doris said. "Call the Norfolk airport, check the flight manifests—"

Don's cell phone rang. He slipped it out of his suit jacket and answered. "Marshal Smites . . ." His eyes opened wide in surprise. "Yes, sir . . . But we might have a kidnapping here . . . Right, but the kids . . . I understand, but . . . Yes, sir . . . we will." He flipped the phone closed and look at Doris in bewilderment.

"What?" Doris asked.

"We've been ordered to Atlanta."

"The Greenes are there?"

Don shook his head. "No. But get this. We're supposed to go down to Atlanta, check into a hotel, and act like we're guarding them. No one's to know they skipped. They're sending doubles to the hotel to make sure it looks good."

"Who was on the phone?" Doris asked.

"The Attorney General of the United States," Don answered, barely able to believe it himself.

23

Joanne paced, watched videos, and napped. Jack tried to read a Western, but couldn't concentrate. The walls seemed to be closing in on him, and with each passing minute, he grew more anxious. To keep himself occupied, he started to examine every square inch of their underground box.

"What are you doing?" Joanne asked from the sofa.

"Looking for a way out."

"The way out is through that locked door. You're driving me crazy! Just give it up."

"That's the problem," Jack said.

"Now what are you talking about?"

"Giving up," Jack said. "Giving in. That's exactly what they expect us to do."

"What choice do we have?"

"We can fight back."

"How?"

127

Jack shrugged. "I don't know yet, but I found a set of butcher knives in the kitchen."

"You're not suggesting—"

"No, I'm not," Jack interrupted. "If Snake Eyes got a knife away from me—and I think she could—she'd cut me into little pieces. But here's a question for you: why would our kidnappers leave a set of sharp butcher knives in our cell?"

"To cut up vegetables," Joanne said.

"Very funny, but you know what I mean."

"I guess it is a little strange," she admitted.

"And look at this furniture." He pointed to the sofa and chairs. "I mean, it's ugly, but it's not cheap. It's the same in the bedrooms—high-quality stuff, expensive, all the comforts of home."

"Like a luxury spider hole," Joanne said.

"What?"

"You know, that hole in the ground in Iraq where they found Saddam Hussein. He had a house above, but when the military was in the area poking around, he went into his hole in the ground and hid until they left. That's why it took so long to catch him."

"Exactly. But this is a lot nicer than the hole they found him in. This isn't a prison." He walked over to one of the tables and pointed underneath. "There's a phone jack here. This is a hideout."

"What difference does it make?" Joanne said. "We're still trapped."

"Exactly," Jack said. "Trap." He was about to elaborate, when the door opened.

By Jack's watch, Snake Eyes was about eight hours early for the photo, and she wasn't alone. A man stepped into the room behind her. He was over six feet tall, a little overweight, with a thick, black, handlebar mustache, and two, mean, dark little eyes darting around the room like a couple of flies.

But the strangest thing about him was the way he was dressed. He looked as though he had stepped out of one of the cowboy videos on the shelf. He was wearing snakeskin boots, a gun belt around his thick waist with ivory-handled pistols and a bowie knife sheathed to it, a pearl snap-button cowboy shirt, and a red kerchief around his neck. He topped off the outfit with a big black cowboy hat. Jack thought it was some kind of joke, but Snake Eyes and the man were not smiling.

Jack and Joanne retreated to the sofa, thinking Snake Eyes had changed her mind about the timing of the next photo, but no camera came out.

Jack glanced at the door. As she had the first time she came in, Snake Eyes left the keys in the lock and the door wide open. He wondered how long it would take to run out, slam the door, and lock it behind them. Too long, he thought.

The man's eyes continued to fly around the room, then they landed on Jack and stayed. "My name is Raphael Aznar," he said with a poor imitation of Texas drawl.

Raphael, Jack thought. The only person Diablo likes. He would not have guessed in a million years that this was Alonzo's brother. About the only thing they had in common was dark hair.

Raphael turned his attention to Joanne. "Alonzo said you were pretty," he commented, then said something to Snake Eyes in Spanish. They both laughed.

He switched back to English. "I was telling her maybe I should pay you a visit some night." He cupped her chin. "How would you like that?"

Joanne started trembling. Jack wanted to string him up by a rope and hang him, and was about to give it a try, when Raphael took his filthy hand away from his sister's face and focused his attention back on Jack.

"Alonzo says your father was keeping a diary."

Jack tried to look confused. It didn't work. Raphael grabbed him by the shirt and yanked him to his feet.

"We know you were the last one to see it," he said, inches from Jack's face. "Where is it?"

Jack shook his head.

Raphael dragged him over to the wall and smacked his head against it. "Either you tell me or I start working on your sister with my knife."

Snake Eyes had moved behind the sofa and was holding Joanne down by the shoulders.

"You want that?" Raphael shouted.

"No."

"Tell me."

"My dad has it," Jack said.

"He didn't give it to the marshals?"

"No."

"Where's he keeping it?"

"I don't know." Jack wasn't about to help them by telling the truth.

130

Raphael tightened his grip and slammed Jack against the wall again.

"If I knew I'd tell you." The edges of Jack's vision were starting to blur. "I don't care about the diary. We just want to get out of here and go home. I don't know where it is."

"How do you know he hasn't given it to the police?"

"He told me that he had it someplace safe. That if something happened to us, he was going to give it to the police."

"Well, something's happened," Raphael said, letting him go. "But something much worse is going to happen if he doesn't give us that diary."

Jack slid down the wall. He thought he might be sick.

Raphael walked over to Joanne. "I look forward to seeing you again." He gave her a feral grin and ran a finger down her cheek, then he and Snake Eyes walked out.

Joanne was off the sofa and across the room before the door closed. "Are you okay?"

Jack sat up. "I think so." But he was dizzy and his stomach was still lurching.

Joanne helped him to his feet. "What's this diary he was talking about?"

Jack was surprised by the question. His mother and Joanne were very close, more like girlfriends than mother and daughter. He thought they shared everything, but apparently his mom hadn't told Joanne about the diary. He explained what it was.

When he finished, she started pacing angrily back and forth across the room.

"So all this is about some stupid diary Dad kept?"

"I guess," he said, but he suspected there was more to it than that.

"What's in this diary?"

"I only saw a couple of pages of it," Jack answered vaguely. "Stuff about Alonzo's drug cartel."

Joanne burst into tears. "Well, I hope Dad gives it to them!" She ran into her bedroom and slammed the door before Jack could share his latest worry.

Raphael had told them who he was. He would not have done that unless it didn't matter. He was not going to let them go.

Day Five

THE VINEYARD

24

Patricia sat next to Sam in the seats directly behind the bulk-head. Smitty was flying. Neil was lying down in the back, getting some badly needed sleep.

They were somewhere over southern Mexico, heading toward a refueling and supply stop in Panama, when the e-mail arrived.

Patricia ignored the message and opened the attached photo, which was four hours old.

"What are they doing to them?" she asked, in shock. "Jack is naked."

"Not quite naked," Sam said. "And he's alive, which is the important thing. Let's look at the e-mail."

They read it together.

Subject: No subject
From: alonzo@network.com
To: osborne@network.com

El Sereno tells me you are reluctant to turn a certain item over to us. I am very sorry to hear this.

If you do not tell us where it is, one of your children will die. You have ten minutes to answer this e-mail.

A.

Patricia gasped and jumped out of her seat. Sam put a firm hand on her arm and shook his head.

"I have to wake Neil," she said, trying to pull away. "We have only ten minutes before the reply address is gone."

"There's nothing he can do," Sam said quietly. "The diary is a thousand miles away from here. Even if you wanted to turn it over to Alonzo, you wouldn't be able to. Let Neil sleep. He'll need his rest."

"But Joanne and Jack—"

"Sit down, Patricia," Sam said. "This is the last e-mail we are going to open from Alonzo. We are no longer going to play his game. We'll answer it, but first, you need to hear me out."

Reluctantly, Patricia sat.

Sam locked his blue eyes on her. "Alonzo Aznar is not going to let your children go, regardless of what you do. Ever. He will keep them alive only as long as he needs them. Then he will kill them. Eventually, he will kill you and Neil as well. He'll do this whether he goes to prison or not. He will not forgive. He will not forget."

Patricia stared at him, letting his words sink in, trying to control her panic. "Why?" she asked. "What could he possibly gain?"

"Retribution," Sam said. "If Alonzo fails to punish you,

the people who work for him will no longer fear him; he will no longer be in control, and eventually, someone will come along and kill him."

"We'll never be safe as long as he's alive," Patricia said bitterly.

"It's not as bad as all that," Sam said, softening a bit. "We'll get your children back. Then we'll deal with Alonzo."

"If we don't kill him, I don't see—"

"Sometimes the threat of death is worse than death," Sam interrupted. "You leave Alonzo to me." He looked at his watch. "If you'll allow me, I'd like to respond to his e-mail."

"All right," Patricia said.

Subject: Re: No Subject
From: osborne@network.com
To: alonzo@network.com

I have the diary with me. Unfortunately, Patricia and I are with the marshals in Atlanta, getting ready for the trial. They came to Manteo last night and put us in protective custody before I could get it to you.

I will give you the diary when I can.

I will change my testimony.

I will do whatever you ask.

It may be difficult to respond to these e-mails quickly, with the U.S. Marshals watching us. I was lucky to get this one out.

No more threats. You've won, but if you harm my children, I swear to God, I will give the diary to the marshals and I will NOT change my testimony.

Neil

Patricia read over what Sam had written, then gave him a grim nod. He hit the SEND button, with five minutes to spare, and gave the handheld back to her. She stood up and put it in one of the overhead compartments so she wouldn't be tempted to look at it again. Sam nodded in approval.

"Give me a reason to believe that you know what you're doing," she said. "Tell me who you really are, Sam."

He patted the seat next to him and she sat down.

"The short version," he said. "I was born and raised in Saint Petersburg, Russia. A boy with a good ear for music and language. Unfortunately, I was not good enough to make a living as a musician, so I fell back on my second love, languages.

"At the university, my abilities came to the attention of the KGB, which was the Soviet equivalent of your Central Intelligence Agency. I became a spy. For over twenty years I plied my trade throughout Europe, Southeast Asia, South America, the Middle East, and the United States. I loved the work and I was good at it, but something bad happened late in my career.

"During an assignment, my son became ill. They would not tell my wife where I was, nor did they tell me he was sick. By the time I got home, he was dead and buried. My wife had divorced me."

"I'm so sorry," Patricia said.

"It was a long time ago," he said. "I resigned from the KGB. Not a healthy thing to do back then. I knew a little too much for the Soviet government's comfort. Things that would be very embarrassing to our country if they were to get out."

Sam shook his head. "Intelligence organizations are notoriously paranoid. I would have never divulged any of their secrets, but my bosses at the KGB didn't trust me and decided that I was a liability. They tried to kill me."

"So you came here," Patricia said.

Sam nodded. "I had no choice but to defect. And the United States was delighted to have me. I spent nearly three years in Washington, D.C., being debriefed. I told them only a fraction of what I really knew, and nothing terribly important, but they were pleased. When they were finished with me, I was offered positions at the CIA, private and public think tanks, and the National Security Agency. But I turned all the offers down. Instead, I asked for a truck, gas money, and to be left alone. I drove across the United States, taking my time, stopping here and there. Eventually, I ended up in Elko."

"So they just let you go?" Patricia asked. "No strings attached?"

"There are always strings," Sam answered. "But the strings they put on me were rather loose and easy to live with. I'd get calls from time to time, asking for advice. Sometimes agents would drop by the Nevada Hotel to ask my opinion about this or that. I didn't mind. It allowed me to keep my fingers in things. One of which was helping the U.S. Marshal Service with witness security. That was how I got in to see Neil when he was in jail."

"Did you have any influence over him getting released?" Patricia asked. Both she and Neil thought it odd they had let him out so easily.

"Not really," Sam answered.

"And getting the marshals to back off?"

"For certain."

"And the classified information about Neil?"

"That's a little more complicated," Sam said. "How much has he told you about what he did before he became a fighter pilot?"

"I knew he was a Navy SEAL," Patricia answered. "I think he would have told me more, but the truth is, I didn't really want to know the specifics. I guess I'm somewhat of a pacifist. This macho, you kill us, we'll kill you stuff, seems ridiculous to me. There has to be a better way."

"Sometimes there is a better way," Sam said. "And sometimes there isn't. That's when Neil and his team were sent in. The reason he was let out of jail before the trial was because of who he was, not because of me. Neil was very good at what he used to do—some say he was the best. When he told you that he and Smitty could handle this situation, he was telling the truth. In fact, he probably could get Jack and Joanne back without Smitty's help or mine."

Patricia thought about this for a few moments, remembering when she and Neil got married. He was gone more than he was home. The long absences almost ended their marriage. She told him that she could not live that way. Neil took care of it. He was qualified to fly a half dozen different aircraft. He talked the Navy into letting him become a fighter pilot. Joanne was born and they moved from base to base for a few years. Patricia wanted a permanent home. Neil took care of that too. He resigned his commission and got a job with the airlines, which went fine for a few years, but then he got restless.

"What I still don't understand," she said, "is how Neil could have worked for someone like Alonzo Aznar?"

"I bet he doesn't understand it either," Sam said. "But it might have something to do with living on the edge for so many years. Not knowing if this would be the day you die. Where everything you do matters. It's a potent tonic, addictive. Believe me, I know. Neil would not be the first person to fail the transition to a so-called normal life, where the most critical decision you have to make on a long weekend is what brand of fertilizer you're going to put on your lawn.

"I also believe if Neil hadn't been arrested he would have come to his senses on his own. He would have taken Alonzo down. That's where he was headed before he was arrested."

Patricia looked doubtful.

"I'm not saying this to make you feel better," Sam said. "The DEA has been trying to infiltrate Alonzo's cartel for years. Neil was able to get inside in a matter of weeks."

"He did it for the money," Patricia said. "By his own admission."

"I'm certain he did," Sam said. "At least at first. And that's the only way he could have gotten in. If he had been undercover with the DEA, Alonzo would have figured it out right away. He's smart about people. That's why he's been around so long.

"I think Neil's motivation started to shift. He began to write things down. When he started the diary he was back in the game. Going after the bad guys. When all the pieces were in place, he would have moved against Alonzo. They arrested him before he gave himself the chance."

Patricia was still not totally convinced, but there was some truth to what Sam was saying.

"What about you?" she asked. "At The Nevada you mentioned that you were living in a different country."

"France," Sam said. "I've been brought out of retirement."

"To do what?

"I think it best if we save the answer to that for another conversation," Sam said. "Before all this happened, I was going to try to get in touch with you."

"Really?"

Sam nodded. "I wanted to talk to you about an opportunity that would allow you to become the Osborne family again—permanently. Something that would help Neil to find himself."

"I'm all ears," Patricia said. "I'd do just about anything to keep the Osborne family together."

"It wouldn't be without risks. But keeping a family together is worth a lot of risk." Sam glanced at his watch. "I'll tell you all about it, but first I need to check on some things."

Patricia watched him walk to the back of the airplane. He had been making and receiving calls and using his computer throughout the long flight. Who was Sam Sebesta, really?

El Sereno sat in a car across the street from the Greenes and watched the two U.S. Marshals go in and come back out of the house. He recognized them as Doris Welty and Don Smites, the Osborne's handlers. Why are they here? And why did they leave so quickly?

He wrote down the license plate number of their rental car as they drove away. With that, he could find out all he needed to know about where the marshals were going.

Alonzo had sent him to Manteo to retrieve Neil Osborne's diary, confident that Neil would turn it over to them now that they had his children.

El Sereno watched the house from his car for ten more minutes. When no one else came out, he walked across the street and peered through one of the side windows for another ten minutes. The Osbornes were not at home. He picked the lock on the back door. Inside, he made a quick search, finding the same evidence the marshals had found. The Osbornes had packed some things and looked like they had left in a hurry.

He made a call to a friend and gave him the marshals' license plate number. Five minutes later, his friend called back. Marshals Welty and Smites had flown down from Washington, D.C., to Norfolk earlier that day and just moments ago, they booked a flight from Norfolk to Atlanta.

He e-mailed Alonzo the information. The reply came back almost immediately. Alonzo told him to go to Atlanta and find out what the marshals were up to.

By the time the e-mail arrived, El Sereno was already on his way.

Alonzo nearly threw the handheld against the cinder block wall when he got Neil Osborne's reply about the diary. He did not like to be threatened, and he was not used to people dictating terms to him.

Subject: No Subject
From: alonzo@overt.com
To: raphael@overt.com

We have some trouble here. I will give you the details when I find out more. Neil is not fully cooperating and may need more incentive. Before the next photo, have Zita work the boy over so Neil knows we are serious.

And give me an update on how preparations are proceeding for the meeting.

A.

Alonzo had a highly developed sixth sense, which had saved his life on numerous occasions. He could feel trouble coming. And he felt the prickly sensation now, moving up his spine like a spider.

27

Jack listened to Joanne crying in the bedroom for a long time, and felt terrible. He wished there were something he could say to make her feel better, but the truth was, nothing he said would change the fact that they were locked up in a concrete bunker with a maniac cowboy threatening to pay her a visit.

He went into the bathroom to check in the mirror for damage and realized that he now had two bumps on his head—one on front and one on back. Two things were obvious: it would be a while before he'd be wearing his baseball cap, and, in order to get out of here, he would have to use his head for something other than a battering ram.

When he came out of the bathroom, Jack noticed how heavy the door was. He took a closer look and saw it was made out of a solid slab of hardwood. The other thing he noticed was that the door was hung wrong. His father had taught him that doors were always hung to swing in when you enter a room and pull closed when you leave.

This gave him an idea. He went back into the bathroom and was happy to see that the glass shower stall was opaque, perfect for what he had in mind. Next, he went to the utility room. On the shelf above the washer and dryer was a toolbox with a couple of screwdrivers, a tape measure, wrenches, a small saw, a hammer, and some other odds and ends. Everything he would need.

In the corner of the room was a broom. He sawed the wooden handle off, then cut it into small sections. In the kitchen he used a hammer, chisel, and paring knife to whittle the sections into shims.

Next, he went into his bedroom. There was a long wooden shelf above the clothes rack. He took it out, measured it, then cut off the end. He brought both pieces into the living room and nailed the small piece he had cut off onto the floor in back of the sofa.

The piece stuck out like a sore thumb, and he was trying to decide how to disguise it, when Joanne stepped out of her bedroom, with red, swollen eyes.

"It's three o'clock in the morning," she said. "What are you doing?"

"Remodeling."

"I'm in no mood for your jokes."

Jack knew he couldn't pull this off on his own. In fact, it would be pointless to try unless Joanne was with him one hundred percent. He explained what he had in mind, and he had to hand it to her, she listened to the whole plan without a word before she came totally unglued.

148

"You are out of your mind!"

"It will work," he insisted.

"Suppose it does," Joanne said. "Then what?"

Jack didn't have an answer. All he knew was they couldn't just sit inside the bunker and wait for some miracle to happen. And being trapped underground was really getting on his nerves. He was beginning to think that he had claustrophobia.

"As soon as Dad gives them that stupid diary they'll let us go," Joanne said.

Jack shook his head. "I don't think this is just about the diary. If it were they wouldn't have flown us all the way down here. There's more to this than we know. A lot more."

"I still say we wait it out," Joanne insisted.

Jack took a deep breath. He didn't want to bring up this next argument, but she wasn't leaving him any choice.

"Raphael is coming back," he said quietly. "Maybe today."

Joanne shuddered in revulsion. "We could barricade the door," she said.

"I already thought about that," Jack said. "They'll cut the power and water. The food will run out. All it would do is to delay the inevitable. We've got to get out of here."

Joanne spent a minute or two looking at Jack's preparations, then turned to him and said, "We've got four hours. We better go over this again."

28

Smitty leveled out at two hundred feet above the thick jungle canopy. It was nearly impossible to see in the dark, with the mist rising above the trees.

"Are you sure this is right?" he asked Neil through his headset.

Sitting in the copilot's seat, Neil checked the coordinates again. "Affirmative. The strip should be about fifteen miles ahead."

"And you think this Sam guy knows what he's doing? I mean, we could have landed at a regular airport to fuel up."

"You're the one who vouched for him back in Elko," Neil pointed out.

An hour earlier, Sam had come into the cockpit and told them that they were being met at a secret landing strip to pick up a passenger and some supplies.

Smitty glanced at the fuel gauge. "Well, if he's wrong,

and there's no place to land, we're going to be putting the jet down anyway. We're flying on fumes."

"He said they'd have fuel." But Sam hadn't said who "they" were, Neil thought, leaning forward, trying to see through the misty darkness.

"There!" Neil said. "Lights at three o'clock."

"Got it."

Smitty banked the jet toward the light. As they drew closer, they saw that the lights were actually coming from vehicles—four, all together—one parked on either end of the crude runway and one on either side.

"It's long and wide enough," Smitty said, switching on the landing lights.

He lined up with the scar cut into the jungle, lowered the landing gear, and came in for his final approach. The grass runway was not nearly as soft as it looked. He managed to make a near-perfect landing, and taxied to the end of the runway.

"Swing it around," Neil said. "In case we have to make a quick exit."

"We don't have enough fuel to make it to the other end of the runway," Smitty said with a laugh, but he brought the Learjet around anyway.

The vehicles started moving toward them, and they were happy to see that one of them was a fuel truck.

"I guess they're going to let us take off again." Smitty shut the engines down.

Sam already had the door open by the time Neil and Smitty came out of the cockpit. A tall, muscular man in army fatigues stepped into the airplane.

151

"Evening, folks," he said. "Which one of you is Commander Osborne?"

Neil was shocked. "They" were the United States Army. Not only that, the officer's shoulder patch—a black unsheathed dagger against a red background—indicated he was an elite Delta Force operator, the army's answer to the navy SEALs.

"I'm Osborne."

"Captain Winters." He gave Neil a salute. "We have most everything you wanted, sir."

Neil looked at Sam, but the custodian gave nothing away.

The captain pulled a list out of his pocket and started reading.

"A couple M4A1's with ammo, sound suppressors, laser sites, and grenade launchers. A few blocks of C-4 and a roll of M700 fuse. Two assault vests. A pile of flex cuffs. Two pair of night-vision goggles. Half a dozen XM84 stun grenades. Three M26 taser pistols. Some smoke grenades. Five LASH radio headsets. And a complete medical pack."

With each item, Smitty's grin grew broader. "That oughta do'er, Captain," he said.

Patricia did not know what half the items were, but they all sounded lethal, except for the medical pack, which worried her most of all.

"Thanks," Neil said, still slightly stunned.

"I'd better go out and check on the refueling," Smitty said.

"I'll go with you," Captain Winters offered, starting to follow him out. "I'll have my men put your supplies on board."

"Excuse me, Captain," Sam interrupted.

152

The Captain stopped.

"There should be some more supplies," Sam said. "And another passenger."

Captain Winters grinned. "He's here, but he's not too happy. We had to drop him in by a tandem parachute to get him here on time. Guess he's never jumped before. The army ranger he was hooked to said he screamed all the way down. And it didn't help when they got hung up in a tree. Our medic's giving him some tranquilizers."

Sam laughed. "I suspect he has a bag of tranquilizers himself."

"He brought along a lot more than a bag," Captain Winters said. "Never seen so much stuff. But he was in no condition to do anything for himself when we cut him down. I'd never seen anyone shake like that. I thought he was having some kind of seizure. But then again, I've never seen anyone jump out of a airplane wearing a suit and tie, either."

"I'd better go out and tend to him," Sam said.

After they left, Neil looked at Patricia. "How are you holding up?"

"I'm fine," she answered. "What was that all about?"

"You'll have to ask Sam. He appears to be in charge of this operation." He put his arm around her. "Any more messages?"

"I turned it off and stowed it in one of the overheads. No point in looking at it if we can't answer."

Neil kissed her. "Our chances for getting them back are a lot better with the things Sam's managed to scrounge. This is all very familiar territory for me."

"Have you ever done a hostage rescue?" Patricia asked.

"Hundreds of times in practice, three times for real."

"Did you lose anyone?"

"Nope."

Soldiers started handing supplies through the door. When they finished, Smitty came back on board, followed by Sam and his mysterious passenger, who was as far removed from a Delta operator as a human could possibly be. He was small—not much over five feet—old, and frail, as if he might break if he fell, which he seemed on the verge of doing, as Captain Winters and Smitty helped him up the stairs. As the captain reported, he was wearing a suit—gray pinstriped—torn at the knees and lapel. His long thinning white hair stuck straight up in places and was sprinkled with jungle debris. The thick wire-rim glasses perched on the end of his rather large nose were twisted, and fogged with Panamanian mist.

"This is an old friend of mine," Sam said. "Dr. Igor Pavlov."

Dr. Pavlov looked at everyone in turn, then said something to Sam in what sounded like Russian.

Sam responded in the same language, then led him over to one of the seats in back. Dr. Pavlov belted himself in, removed his glasses, reclined the seat, and closed his eyes.

"He's had a harrowing experience," Sam said. "He'll be fine after a rest."

Everyone on the jet, except for Sam, doubted this, and wondered why Dr. Pavlov had been brought on board; but there was no time to discuss it.

"You're all fueled up," Captain Winters said. "Oh, one other thing." He handed Neil a plastic mailing tube.

"What's this?"

"Don't know. It was with the supplies." Captain Winters gave him a salute and closed the door to the Learjet.

Neil opened the tube. Inside was a complete set of plans for the Aznar Vineyards and satellite photos of the property dated the day before.

"This will be helpful," he said, looking at Sam.

"More than you think," Sam said, taking the satellite images.

"What's our next move?" Smitty asked.

"We fly to Santiago, Chile," Sam said. "Then on to the vineyard."

Neil frowned. "Why not just go straight to the vine-yard?"

"Because they're not expecting us until early this evening."

"Expecting us?" Neil shouted.

Sam ignored the outburst and turned to Patricia. "What size jeans do you wear?" he asked.

29

El Sereno arrived in Atlanta by private jet, two and a half hours before Marshals Doris Welty and Don Smites. By the time he got there he knew the hotel and room they would be staying in.

He reserved the room directly above theirs and got settled in as his surveillance crew installed miniature cameras and sophisticated listening devices in the marshals' double suite.

Just as the sun was coming up, he watched the thoroughly exhausted marshals come into the room and drop their bags. Don barely had time to loosen his tie and remove his suit jacket before there was a knock on the door.

Doris looked through the peephole, then opened the door, letting in a man and a woman resembling Neil and Patricia Osborne.

"Is that them?" one of his crew asked.

El Sereno shook his head no and e-mailed Alonzo.

As he waited for Alonzo's reply, his cell phone rang. On the other end was a voice from his past. A voice he never thought he would hear again.

The man on the other end said his name was Sam Sebesta. But El Sereno knew him by another name.

30

Zita Vega was looking forward to this morning's photo session. She did not like the boy and thought Raphael had been too lenient with him the day before. Today he would get a proper beating, one that would convince Neil Osborne to turn the diary over to them.

Three stablemen were in the barn when she came in. She shouted for them to leave. The men obeyed without hesitation, leaving their pitchforks standing in the stalls they were mucking out.

She slammed the door behind them and strode over to Diablo's stall. Even he sensed that today was not a good day to resist the woman with the strange eyes. He stood perfectly still, sweating, as she jerked a halter over his ears and tied him to the post in the stall. He jumped at the sound of the secret door opening and looked back, relieved to see the woman disappearing into the darkness.

Zita glanced at her watch. Five after seven. Her plan was to handcuff both of them, then beat the boy in front of his sister. When she opened the door, she saw that Joanne was alone on the sofa. She didn't need one, but now Zita had a very good reason to beat the boy. She had told them to be ready.

"Where is he?"

"He's taking a shower," Joanne said, clearly frightened. "He'll be out in a minute."

He'll be out in five seconds, Zita thought as she jerked the girl's arms behind her back, snapping on a pair of cuffs as tight as they would go.

The bathroom door was closed and she could hear the shower on the other side. If the boy had locked the door, she would kill him, she decided. Alonzo wouldn't like it, but they still had the girl, and the plan was to eventually kill both of them anyway.

The door was unlocked and she felt a tinge of disappointment as she pulled it open. She strode over to the shower stall and jerked the door open. It was empty.

31

Jack ran out of the bedroom, where he had been hiding, and slammed the bathroom door behind Snake Eyes. A second later she hit the other side of the door like wrecking ball, jarring every bone in his body.

"Get the board I cut!" he shouted at Joanne. "We have to wedge the door closed!"

"I can't!"

He glanced back at her and swore when he saw that her hands were cuffed behind her. "Help me lean against it!"

Joanne ran over and put her shoulder against the door. Jack pulled the hammer and screwdriver from under his belt.

Bam! Snake Eyes hit the door again with an enraged scream. The door moved, but they were able to keep it closed.

Jack wedged the screwdriver between the door and the

jamb and hit it with the hammer a second before Snake Eyes made her third run. The door did not move as much as it had the second time. He gave the screwdriver another whack, then pulled the shims out of his pocket and started hammering them in. With each one, the door became more solid, either that or Snake Eyes was losing her strength.

Jack told Joanne to keep leaning against the door while he got the board he had hidden under the sofa. He wedged one end under the doorknob and put the other end against the board he had nailed to the floor.

"I hope that holds her," he said.

"I hope so, too," Joanne said. "What about these?" She turned around and showed him the handcuffs.

Jack retrieved the key ring Snake Eyes had left dangling in the front door. On it was a small handcuff key. He unlocked Joanne's cuffs.

Snake Eyes was still yelling and pounding on the door. Jack prayed that the bunker was as soundproof as it appeared to be. And that the two-way radio she was carrying didn't work underground.

"How long do you think we have?" Joanne asked, rubbing the feeling back into her wrists.

"Until someone comes down here and sets her free. They'll have to use a chisel to get the shims out. It will take them a while."

What Jack didn't know was how long it would be before Snake Eyes was missed. He went into the bedroom and got his pack, which he had stuffed with food, water, and other things he thought they might need.

"Ready?"

"I guess," Joanne answered uncertainly.

They stepped through the doorway, and Jack was about to lock the door behind them, but hesitated.

"Hang on." He went back inside and got the hammer.

"Now what are you doing?" Joanne asked.

Instead of answering, he locked the door, then hit the key with the hammer, breaking it off in the lock.

"That ought to slow them down." He put the other keys in his pocket.

32

As Joanne and Jack made their way up the stairs to the secret door, Alonzo Aznar paced his small cell like a circus cat waiting to be let into the ring.

The Osbornes were not in Atlanta, although the marshals wanted it to appear that they were. El Sereno had been able to trace them as far as the Dallas/Fort Worth airport, but from there it was a dead end. The Watcher was still monitoring the marshals in their suite, but so far that had yielded nothing. But the thing that really infuriated Alonzo was the three e-mails he had sent to Neil demanding to know where he was had gone unanswered. This kind of disrespect could not be tolerated. Neil would be taught a lesson he would never forget.

Alonzo typed a simple message to his brother on the handheld:

Kill the boy now.

A moment after he sent it, one of the inmates he had hired stopped by his cell.

"What do you want?"

"Just checking in on you," the inmate said. "You haven't been down to the cafeteria for two days."

"So?"

"Thought you might be hungry." He held up a Burger King bag.

Alonzo was suspicious. "Where did you get it?"

"One of the guards," the inmate said. "He stops on his way in and picks it up. Charges twice what it costs, but it's better than the slop they serve here. If you're not interested it's no sweat off my back. I'll eat it myself."

"Leave it," Alonzo said.

Jack led the way up the stairs, hoping the barn would be deserted like it had been the day before. It was, except for Diablo, who nearly kicked Jack's head off when he stepped through the secret door. The huge hooves missed him by an inch. He fell backward, knocking Joanne down the stairs and landing on top of her.

"What do you think you're doing?" Joanne shrieked.

"Quiet!" Jack hissed. "There might be people in the barn. The satanic stallion took a swipe at me."

They untangled themselves.

"How are we going to get by him?" Joanne whispered.

"I don't know, but we have to do it quick."

Jack crept back up the stairs to look the situation over. From his vantage point, a couple steps from the top, the stallion looked the size of a tyrannosaurus rex.

Diablo turned his gigantic head and gave Jack a

wide-eyed glare, as if to say: *There's a lot more where that came from. Come on up.*

Jack knew virtually nothing about horses. All he knew was that he and Joanne had to get out of the barn now. He took the pack off and tossed it down the stairs to Joanne.

"Don't come up until I give the okay," he said.

"What are you—"

Jack rushed the stallion, thinking he was going to either get past the beast or his head was going to be the next thing to fly down the stairs. He wasn't exactly sure what happened next, but whatever it was, it hurt. He flew through the air and hit the ground like a bag of rocks, expecting to be trampled to death, but the hooves never came. When he opened his eyes he saw that he was lying on his back in the aisle, with Diablo safely behind the stall door. The wind was knocked out of him, but nothing seemed to be broken.

Slowly, he got to his feet, greatly relieved to see he was still in one piece and that no one was in the barn to witness his flying act.

"Jack?" Joanne called fretfully.

He walked over to the stall. "I'm fine. Stay where you are while I figure out how to get this monster out of the way."

That job turned out to be relatively easy. He simply untied the halter rope and swung the door open. Diablo shot out of the stall like a cannonball, snorting and bucking to the far end of the barn.

"It's clear," Jack said.

Joanne came up carrying the pack. Jack closed the secret door behind her.

"Which way?" Joanne asked.

Jack looked toward Diablo, who was still bucking and chipping wood from the walls with his hooves.

"Not that way." He took the pack from her and led her to the opposite door.

As he reached for the knob, it started to turn from the outside. He grabbed Joanne and pulled her behind the door just as it banged open. Three men came running through, shouting in Spanish. At first he thought they were after them, but it quickly became clear that Diablo was the object of their panic. One of them grabbed a lariat from a hook, and the three of them cautiously advanced toward Diablo, completely unaware of the two fugitives hiding behind them.

Jack waited until Diablo had their full attention, which did not take long. Diablo was enjoying his freedom and was fully prepared to fight the three men to keep it.

When the battle started, Jack and Joanne ran out of the barn and were nearly blinded by the bright morning sun after spending nearly twenty-four hours underground. Joanne came to her senses first and pulled Jack around the corner of the barn, where they hid behind a bush near a fenced paddock.

"What now?" she asked.

Jack couldn't answer right away. He was still a little stunned over the fact that they had gotten as far as they had. Two more men ran by. One of them was shouting something in Spanish into a handheld radio. And, like Raphael, he was decked out from head to toe like a cowboy, with a pair of six-shooters holstered around his waist. Jack hoped he wasn't talking to Snake Eyes.

"Run or hide," Jack finally answered. "Those are our only two choices." He was leaning toward hiding. They wouldn't get very far if they ran. He figured it would take an hour or so for the men to get through the bunker door after they discovered Snake Eyes was missing. The other problem was that it was broad daylight. It would have been better to spring the trap that night, but Jack had the feeling that if he had waited until then it would have been too late.

"Run or hide *where*?" Joanne asked.

Jack didn't know, but they couldn't stay where they were. Another cowboy ran past, but didn't see them.

There were several buildings on their side of the barn, which he hadn't seen when they arrived. On a hill above them was a huge house overlooking the lake they had flown over. Beneath it, along the shore, was a strange sight. A town, right out of the Old West, with clapboard saloons, stores, hotels, a blacksmith shop . . . there was even a church. A horse-drawn supply wagon was bouncing down the dusty block-long street, and there were several horses tied to hitching posts outside the buildings.

"You think they have a marshal?" Jack whispered.

Joanne stared down at the town. "I suppose with their kind of money, the Aznars can indulge any fantasy or build whatever they want. And no, I don't think they have a marshal. How far is Mendoza from here?"

"Fifty miles," Jack said. "Maybe a little more. I vote for finding a place to hide. I don't think they'll expect us to hang around, and we'll have a better chance of getting out of here after dark."

"Okay."

They ran to the nearest building and tried the door. It was locked.

"Try one of the keys," Joanne said.

Jack fished them out, and on the fourth try, found the right one. He opened the door cautiously and looked inside. The lights were off and no one seemed to be around. He pulled Joanne through the door and locked it behind them.

At first glance it looked like some kind of storage building. Hundreds of oak wine barrels were stacked, seven or eight high along the walls, and pallets of oak planks covered the floor. Just above the barrels was a row of dirty windows, letting in just enough light for them to see.

"It's a barrel factory," Jack said, walking over to a long workbench to look at the tools.

Files, mallets, chisels, saws, and metal cutters were not going to help them. He went over to the barrels and discovered they were all empty and easy to move.

"I guess we'll have to make ourselves a little cubby hole and hide in it until dark."

"What about mice?" Joanne asked.

"What about Raphael?"

It was a mean thing to say, but it had the desired effect. She started to help him rearrange the barrels. After ten minutes they had a nice hiding spot hollowed out.

Jack crawled in first, and Joanne joined him after he assured her that there were no mice. At least that he could see.

"How did you get by Diablo?" she asked him.

"He either bucked or kicked me out of the stall. I'm not sure which."

"Well, it was impressive."

"It was desperate," Jack corrected.

34

Raphael Aznar did not wake up until eleven, which was relatively early for him. But he had a lot to do.

The jamboree was tonight. Thirty-five people were flying in to the vineyard for the annual cartel meeting to be held at Durango, the Old West town he had personally designed and built—authentic, from the tar on the roofs to the brass spittoons beneath the saloon bars.

He stepped out onto the bedroom balcony, with a cup of black coffee, looking down on Durango. Preparations for the jamboree were well underway, with supplies being brought in by horse-drawn wagons and handcarts.

Motorized vehicles were not allowed in the town, nor were electricity, phones, two-way radios, automatic weapons, synthetic clothing, or anything else that did not exist in 1871.

Raphael smiled, remembering their first jamboree several years ago. The guests were not pleased when his men confiscated their weapons and cell phones and made them change into western attire. But their protests quickly passed after they stepped back into time in Durango. The following year everyone showed up wearing the proper clothes, carrying Colt revolvers, Winchester repeaters, and bowie knives.

But this year's jamboree would be different from past years. For the first time, Alonzo would not be here. The brothers had discussed canceling it, or at least delaying it until Alonzo's release, but if they did either, the members of the cartel would become more frantic than they already were.

Each day Alonzo remained in jail, it became increasingly difficult to keep everyone in line. Some were threatening to start their own operations, and Raphael's job tonight was to stop that in its tracks. With the Osborne brats locked up beneath the barn, Alonzo's release was assured.

The face-to-face meetings took place in a back room of one of the saloons. Members of the cartel were brought in, individually or in small groups, and were told what was expected of them in the coming year. Alonzo had stayed in business by completely compartmentalizing the cartel. Each member knew only their piece of the puzzle. If they were arrested they could tell the authorities only about their small part of the overall picture.

This is why Neil Osborne's diary was so important. Somehow, the pilot had managed to gather all the pieces and put them together.

Raphael checked his notes. He had written down on little cards exactly what Alonzo wanted him to tell each cartel member. He hoped it wouldn't take too long, so he could enjoy the party himself.

He walked back inside and took a shower and dressed. It wasn't until he was strapping on his gun belt that he remembered to check the handheld computer. He retrieved it from his dresser and read the message from Alonzo:

Kill the boy now.

Apparently, Zita's beating had not been enough to convince Neil to turn the diary over. He was pleased that Alonzo had chosen for the boy to die first, and not the girl. He had plans for her.

He called Zita on the radio and was surprised and irritated when she didn't answer. That wasn't like her. Downstairs he asked the servants if they had seen her, but nobody had since early that morning.

Now he was angry. He didn't have time for this. He barked out several orders to his staff about the jamboree, then stamped out of the house. When he got to the barn he asked a stable hand if he had seen Zita.

"Early this morning she told us to leave the barn," he explained nervously. "Later we heard kicking noises from inside and found Diablo loose. We had a terrible time getting him back into his stall. Señorita Zita was not there."

Raphael, alarmed now, shoved him out of the barn and slammed the door closed.

Diablo nickered like a young colt when he saw him. Raphael walked over to the stall and pulled several sugar cubes out of his pocket and gave them to him.

"What happened here this morning? Did you battle the men?"

172

Raphael opened the door and Diablo stepped out as calm as an old draft horse. "Alonzo will be back soon," he said, slipping a halter over Diablo's head without a fuss. "Then you and I will resume our old life. I'm as sick of staying in the house as you are of being in the stall."

He tied Diablo to a post, then opened the secret passage and walked down the stairs.

The first thing he noticed was the hammer lying in front of the door. He picked it up, wondering if Zita had used it on the boy. Perhaps she had gotten carried away and killed him, and now she was afraid to answer the radio. Orders were to be carried out exactly as described—no more, no less. He hoped she had not gone totally loco and killed the girl, too.

Raphael tried to slip his key into the lock and found that it would not go in. He bent down for a closer look and saw what the hammer had really been used for.

He ran back up the stairs and tried to reach Zita on the radio again. She didn't answer. He grabbed a handful of tools.

After twenty infuriating minutes of trying to get the broken key out of the lock, he gave up and used a sledgehammer to smash the lock off the door.

Out of breath, he drew his revolver, cocked it, and ran into the room, praying the kids were still there.

They weren't.

He looked down at the board wedged against the bathroom door and threw it across the room, shattering the television screen. It took him another half hour to chisel enough wedges out of the jamb for Zita to be able to kick the

173

door open. When she did, it hit him in the forehead and knocked him down.

Raphael was so angry he reached for his pistol, and the only thing that stopped him from drawing was the look of contorted rage on Zita's face. One of the snake contacts had popped out, giving her two different-colored eyes. He thought she might explode right then and there, and he scooted backward so he would not get hit by the carnage.

She let out a demonic scream that froze his blood and made every hair on his body stand on end. When she finished, she picked up one of the heavy leather chairs and threw it halfway across the room. She closed her eyes and took a deep breath.

"What time is it?" she asked, considerably calmer.

Raphael got to his feet and looked at his pocket watch. "Noon."

He wanted to ask her how she had been duped by two children, but thought better of it. Instead, he told her about Alonzo's latest instructions and asked if she had beaten the boy before they escaped.

"No," she said. "But I look forward to killing them both."

"With a five-hour head start," Raphael pointed out, "that could be a problem."

"We'll organize a search team," Zita said.

There was nothing Raphael would rather do than set up a posse and ride them down, but there were a couple of problems with the plan. First, no one at the vineyard was supposed to know the Osborne kids were there. Second, everyone was getting ready for the jamboree, which was only a few hours away. He explained the problems to Zita.

"Obviously," she said, "we'll have to alert everyone on the vineyard, and we'll have to cancel the jamboree."

Raphael shook his head. "We'll tell only a trusted few until we find out what Alonzo wants us to do. And it's too late to cancel the jamboree. People are already on their way here from as far away as Japan, the U.S., and Europe."

"You're a fool!" Zita said bitterly, running out of the room and up the stairs.

I'm a fool? Raphael thought, following her out. I'm not the one who allowed two children to escape. He found her in the barn checking her e-mail on the handheld.

There were five messages from Alonzo. Each one more insistent that she e-mail him an update.

"Are you going to tell him the kids are gone?" Raphael asked. "Or do you want me to do it?"

"I'll do it."

She typed the message in and hit the SEND button with dread.

Alonzo was in no condition to receive the message. He was in the back of an ambulance, with sirens blaring and lights flashing, on his way to the county hospital.

Around noon he'd begun to feel a tightening in his chest and shortness of breath. At first he thought it was indigestion from the food the inmate had brought him, or some kind of adverse reaction to the stress he had been under the past few days.

It was neither. Alonzo Aznar was having a heart attack.

He stumbled out of his cell and called out for help. The two inmates and the guards came running. Ten minutes later the paramedics arrived and rushed him out of the jail, strapped to a gurney.

By the time he arrived at the hospital he had stabilized and insisted that he be taken back to his cell.

The young emergency room doctor shook his head.

"We're keeping you here for at least a couple days, maybe longer. We need to run some tests."

"I want to see my lawyer," Alonzo said.

"I'll let the guards know," the doctor said. "But he's not the one who's going to fix your heart."

36

Neil landed at the Santiago International Airport in Chile, not knowing what to expect. Sam had given them only a rough outline of his plan, promising more details as they got closer to the vineyard.

"A hundred and twenty miles to Mendoza," Smitty said, looking at the aeronautical chart from the copilot seat.

Thanks to Sam they were almost certain that Joanne and Jack had been taken to the vineyard. The satellite photographs showed a jet similar to the one they were in landing at the vineyard yesterday afternoon. That flight had come directly from Los Angeles the night before.

The control tower ordered Neil to taxi the jet to an isolated hangar a quarter of a mile from the terminal building. Waiting for them there was a black limousine. As Neil brought the jet to a stop, two men wearing dark suits and sunglasses got out of the backseat.

"Spooks," Smitty said.

Neil doubted it. They looked more like diplomats than spies, and he hoped they weren't there to shut them down. If they tried, he was going to take off, cross the Andes, and save his kids no matter what they did to stop him.

Sam came around the nose of the aircraft and greeted them. They stood talking for a few moments, then one of the men walked around to the back of the limo and popped the trunk. Inside were shopping bags and a wheelchair.

"Did someone get hurt?" Smitty asked.

"I don't know." Neil unsnapped his harness. "Let's go find out."

At the back of the jet, Sam was handing bags through the doorway to Patricia. Dr. Pavlov, who looked a lot better than he had the last time they saw him, was sipping a cup of black coffee, looking at something on Sam's laptop.

Neil helped Patricia with the last bag as Sam closed the hatch.

"What is all this stuff?" Smitty asked, pointing at the wheelchair.

"Disguises," Sam answered. "Let me tell you what I have in mind."

37

Benjamin Bender walked down the sterile hospital hallway toward Alonzo's room. It was easy to see which one was his client's, with two burly, uniformed policemen standing outside the door. He presented his identification to them and they let him in.

"What took you so long?" Alonzo asked irritably. He was propped up in the bed, with an IV drip attached to his arm and EKG leads taped to his chest beneath a flimsy hospital gown.

"I was in court when you called," Bender lied.

Alonzo glared at him.

The truth was that Bender was actually playing golf and had left his cell phone in the clubhouse locker room, but he was not about to confess this to Alonzo. When his office told him that Alonzo had had a heart attack, he nearly jumped for joy, thinking his problems were over. But his hopes were quickly dashed when he called the hospital and a nurse told him that Alonzo was not only alive, but stable.

Right now, Alonzo looked anything but stable. "When do I get out of here?" he asked.

Bender took a step back from the bed. "In a few days."

The *blips* on the heart monitor increased.

"Did you retrieve my handheld from the jail?"

"They wouldn't let me take anything from your cell," Bender said. "I wouldn't worry about it. Your computer is encrypted; they can't read any of the incoming e-mail."

"That is not the point!" Alonzo shouted.

Bender glanced at the door. "There are two cops posted outside."

Alonzo closed his eyes and took a deep breath. When he opened them, he asked in a much calmer tone, "Did you talk to Raphael?"

Bender shook his head. "I've called him three times, but as usual, he's not answering his cell phone."

"Keep trying," Alonzo said, although he didn't think it would do much good. Raphael would rather carry a rattlesnake in his pocket than a cell phone.

Bender nodded, then said, "On the bright side of things, with you in the hospital there's a good chance that we can get the trial delayed again."

"We don't need the trial delayed," Alonzo said.

"What are you talking about?"

Alonzo proceeded to tell Benjamin Bender more than he cared to know.

38

Jack was not enjoying their hiding place. It was hot and tight. His skin crawled.

Occasionally they heard a truck go by, the squeak of a wheelbarrow tire, people talking in Spanish; but no one appeared to be looking for two escaped kids. It was just another quiet day at the vineyard until the jets started landing.

"Did you hear that?" Jack asked.

"Kind of hard to miss," Joanne said. "The building's still shaking."

She was right. Dust rained down from the high rafters, and the corrugated metal sides and roof rattled like snare drums.

Jack closed his eyes and listened. "It landed," he said.

A couple minutes later a second jet came over.

"What's going on?" Joanne asked.

Jack, desperate to get out of their hiding place, told her that he would find out. He started to scoot the barrels out of the way.

"Wait a second!" Joanne grabbed his arm. "I thought we were going to wait until it got dark."

Jack jerked his arm away. "I changed my mind." He pushed another barrel out.

"Would you just listen!"

"I can't!" He pushed the final barrel out of the way and scrambled out.

Joanne followed him. "Are you crazy?"

Jack was too busy hyperventilating to answer. When he finally caught his breath he looked embarrassed. "I guess I'm claustrophobic," he said.

"Great time to figure that out."

"Tell me about it."

Another jet passed overhead. It had gotten considerably darker in the shop, but there was still light filtering through the high windows.

"It will be two hours before it's dark," Joanne said, adding gently, "We'll have to go back in."

Jack dreaded the idea of crawling back into the dark, confined space, but he knew she was right.

"Okay," he said. "But first I'm going to climb up to those windows and see what's going on outside."

Before Joanne could object, he started climbing, which wasn't easy, with the wine barrels tipping and wobbling all the way up to the twenty-foot-high windows. When he finally reached them, he was covered in sweat and oak dust. He looked down on Joanne, who was staring up at him with her hands on her hips, obviously annoyed. He didn't blame her. If she had pulled a stunt like he just had, he would have been irritated too.

He wiped the dust from the window and was rewarded by a spectacular view of the lake, the Old West town, and in the distance, the airstrip. Parked on the runway were three sleek corporate jets. One of them was off-loading passengers into a white limo.

Zita was having no luck finding the Osborne kids. And the search was not helped by Raphael giving her only six men to look for them.

Mendoza was sixty miles from the vineyard. The only way to get there was along a private road that was gated at the entrance and heavily guarded. She doubted the kids would make it that far, but she sent two men into town in case they did. This left her only four men. Two of them were out in SUVs, searching the road and trails. The other two were patrolling the property in a helicopter.

Zita had taken over one of the hacienda's upstairs bedrooms to coordinate the search effort, but so far there had been little to coordinate.

She was beginning to think the kids had not run at all. That they were still on the vineyard somewhere. If this were the case, recapturing them was going to be difficult.

Aznar Vineyards was a huge complex, with dozens of buildings, and with the keys they had stolen from her, the Osborne children had access to all of them. To find them she would need twice as many people.

If only Alonzo would answer her e-mails, she was sure he would authorize all the help she needed. But so far, he had not responded to any of them, including her first one telling him the children had escaped. She was both relieved and worried about this. Relieved, because she wanted to have the kids in hand before he wrote back, and worried, because it wasn't like Alonzo not to respond immediately.

Downstairs, she heard Raphael ushering another group of guests into the house. So far, about twenty people had arrived. As soon as everyone got there they would be driven down to Durango in horse-drawn wagons.

This was Zita's last chance to get Raphael to listen to reason. Once the jamboree officially started, he would be too busy relaying Alonzo's orders to speak to her.

She came out of the bedroom and looked down onto the grand entry at the mingling guests wolfing down hors d'oeuvres and guzzling Aznar wine. The old hands had already changed into their western attire, the new people were in suits or casual clothes.

Raphael was talking to a group of newcomers, no doubt telling them about the Durango dress code. He snapped his fingers and a servant hurried over. She led the bewildered group away to the wardrobe room, where they would be properly outfitted.

Zita hurried down the stairs and got Raphael's attention. She pulled him into the library and closed the door.

"Well?" he said.

"We haven't found them."

Raphael stared at her, displeased.

"They may have stayed right here on the vineyard," Zita said. "I'll need more help to look for them."

"I've already given you more people than I can spare."

"If we don't find them Alonzo will not get out of jail."

"Alonzo will be released regardless of how the trial comes out. You have my word on that." Raphael gave her a cold smile. "And when he does get out, perhaps even before, he'll deal with your failure to keep two stupid kids locked up."

Zita did not think the Osborne kids were stupid, but she did think the man standing in front of her was. He was also dangerous. Because of this, she did not push him too hard.

"Have you heard from Alonzo?" she asked.

"No." Raphael hadn't checked the little computer since that morning.

"I haven't either," Zita said. "That's not like him."

Raphael frowned. She was right, his brother should have responded to her e-mail. He wondered if he had e-mailed him instead of her. Alonzo may have been so angry about losing the kids, he wanted Raphael to punish Zita for her failing him. He was looking forward to it, if that were the case. Since Alonzo had been arrested, she had become increasingly disrespectful toward him, and Raphael was tired of it.

"You'd better find them," he said, then walked out of the library. Crossing the grand entry quickly, without pausing to talk to anyone, he bounded up the stairs to his bedroom and found the little computer. There were no messages waiting, and he wondered what that meant. Clumsily, he typed in a message to his brother, asking if he had gotten Zita's e-mail about the Osborne kids. It didn't even occur to him to check the cell phone lying on the dresser, with the message light blinking.

Another jet flew over. He stepped out onto the balcony and watched it land. He was expecting three more groups in the next hour; then everyone would be there and the jamboree could start.

40

Two more jets came in while Jack was up on top of the barrels. He knew he should climb back down, but he couldn't make himself do it. He didn't want to crawl back into that cubby hole.

He also knew that Joanne was standing below, getting angrier with each passing minute. He justified staying where he was by telling himself that it was more important to find out who these people were than it was to climb back into their cramped hiding place.

Another jet came in for a landing. He wished he had a pair of binoculars so he could get a closer look at the people getting into the limo. Something big was going on at the vineyard and he thought maybe they could use it to their advantage.

He scooted over to the edge of the barrels to check on

Joanne. Just as he had thought, she was impatiently glaring up at him. He was about to tell her that he was going to stay up there, when the door opened.

Joanne ran, but didn't get more than three steps.

"Stay where you are!" Snake Eyes shouted.

Joanne froze.

Snake Eyes crossed the floor in ten strides. She grabbed Joanne's wrist. In her other hand, she had a small pistol.

"Where's your brother?"

"I don't know."

Snake Eyes bent Joanne's wrist back painfully.

"We got separated," Joanne screeched.

Jack thought about clobbering Snake Eyes with a barrel, but she was standing too close to Joanne. He decided to give himself up. But before he could, Snake Eyes went berserk, screaming, kicking things, and dragging Joanne around as she dodged tumbling barrels.

Jack made a desperate lunge for the rafter, grabbing it a split second before the barrels beneath him crashed to the floor like a rockslide. He dangled there for a moment, then pulled himself up behind a huge exhaust fan coming through the metal roof. He expected to find Joanne and Snake Eyes crushed, but aside from being covered in sawdust, they looked fine.

"I told you he wasn't here," Joanne said, choking.

Snake Eyes angrily kicked more barrels to the side.

Again, Jack considered giving himself up. But how could he help his sister if he was locked up too?

"Where did you get separated?" Snake Eyes asked.

"Outside the barn," Joanne said. "Someone came along.

I went one way, and Jack went the other. I haven't seen him since."

Jack shook his head in wonder. Joanne was a good liar and a great actress. He half believed the story himself. She hadn't once glanced up to give him away.

"How did you get in here?" Snake Eyes asked her.

"Your keys."

"Give them to me."

Jack held his breath. The keys were in his pocket.

"Let me go and I'll find them," Joanne said without hesitation.

"What do you mean?"

"Just before you came in I was hiding behind the barrels. The keys are with my pack, somewhere underneath this mess."

Snake Eyes stared at her, deliberating, then said, "Forget the keys."

Jack let his breath out.

"What was your plan?" Snake Eyes asked.

Joanne looked confused.

Snake Eyes bent her wrist back again. "Your plan!"

"We were going to wait until dark and make our way to Mendoza to get help," Joanne said breathlessly. "If we got separated, we were going to meet at the police station."

Snake Eyes let up on her wrist, unsnapped the two-way radio from her belt, and spoke into it in Spanish. When she returned it to her belt, she gave Joanne a humorless smile.

"I told my men to kill your brother when they find him. The Mendoza police work for us."

Joanne let out an anguished moan, which was convincing enough to broaden Snake Eyes's smile. She pulled her through the debris toward the door.

As they exited, Joanne put her free hand behind her back and waved good-bye.

41

Neil watched nervously from the cockpit as Patricia pushed Sam in the wheelchair toward the white limousine. Dr. Pavlov walked next to them, carrying his leather medical bag. They were all dressed in western clothes. Patricia in tight jeans tucked into red cowboy boots, Sam and Dr. Pavlov in more conservative Sunday-go-to-meetin' clothes.

The only weapon Sam took with them was a taser gun hidden in the false bottom of Dr. Pavlov's medical bag. The wheelchair was equipped with a concealed two-way radio, which Sam could monitor through a wireless earpiece disguised to look like a hearing aid. He would wait to turn the radio on until after they got to Durango in case they were subjected to an electronic sweep at the entrance, which was likely. The Aznars were very security conscious.

This was not at all what Neil had in mind when he decided to go after Joanne and Jack. His plan was to burst into the hacienda about four or five in the morning, heavily armed; capture Raphael, and force him to turn the kids over. Crude, but effective.

The perimeter of the vineyard was well guarded with people, cameras, and electronic motion detectors, but the interior had very little security. Raphael did not like too many people around to see what he was doing. Just like in Alonzo's Colombian compound, the servants, stable hands, and workers had been with Raphael for years. He took good care of them and their families, providing them with houses, a decent wage—there was even a private school for their children. They were virtual prisoners on the vineyard, but no one complained and no one ever left.

The burly limo driver lifted Sam from the wheelchair like he was a child, setting him down in the backseat next to Patricia and Dr. Pavlov. He then pushed the wheelchair to the back of the limo, collapsed it, and put it in the trunk.

Smitty came into the cockpit and they watched as the limo pulled away and headed up to the hacienda.

"You okay?" Smitty asked.

"I'm not happy about Patricia going into the lion's den, if that's what you mean."

"She'll be fine. Sam knows what he's doing and Patricia's tough as nails."

Neil wasn't completely convinced about Sam, but he agreed that Patricia was tough. She had been like steel throughout this whole mess. He just wished Sam hadn't wanted her to accompany him to the jamboree and that she hadn't insisted on going over his objections.

"End of subject," he muttered.

"What?" Smitty asked.

"Never mind. What's going on out there?"

"The other pilots are over at the hangar."

"Yeah. They'll play cards, sleep, eat, tell war stories till their bosses stumble back out of Durango."

"Is that what you used to do?"

Neil shook his head. "I was in the inner circle. Alonzo liked me, for some reason. Trusted me. I slept in the house and met his friends."

"You ever feel bad about taking him down?" Smitty asked quietly.

"No. But I do regret getting Patricia and the kids involved. I wish I'd taken him sooner."

Smitty nodded. "Did Sam talk to you about going to work for him?"

"Yeah," Neil said. "He talked to Patricia, too. Wants her to be his assistant."

"What do you think?"

"I don't know yet. I'll think about it after we get the kids back."

"Might be fun to go after the bad guys again," Smitty said. "Better than flying boxes around. And Sam appears to be more competent than most. In fact, if I didn't know better, I'd say this operation is his way of showing us just how competent he is."

"I was thinking the same thing," Neil said.

Smitty looked at this watch. "We have an hour before we need to head out. I think I'll go over to the hangar and see what kind of scuttlebutt I can pick up."

"Good idea," Neil said. "I'll stay here. Half the pilots in there know who I am. I'll get our gear ready."

Smitty turned to leave, but Neil stopped him.

"I haven't had a chance to thank you," he said.

Smitty grinned. "I wouldn't have missed it for the world."

42

Jack watched through the dusty window as Snake Eyes led Joanne toward the house.

Now that he had been marked for death, he guessed Joanne would be safe for the time being. They would have to keep at least one of them alive to get what they wanted from his father. But he still felt terrible about her getting caught. If he had ignored his claustrophobia and stayed where he was, they'd still be safe. His only consolation was that he had a new plan for getting away from the vineyard. The jets were their ticket out of there. Now all he had to do was to get Joanne away from Snake Eyes. But first he had to figure a way to get down from his perch without breaking his neck, and he had to do it fast. It was getting dark out. Pretty soon he wouldn't be able to see his hand in front of his face.

Jumping was out of the question. It was too far, and the

floor beneath him was covered in splintered barrels. He scooted across the beam to take a closer look at the wall and realized he'd have to be a fly or a gecko to climb down it. Perhaps it's better on the other side, he thought, and inched his way across. By the time he got there, it was considerably darker, and the wall on this side looked just as impossible.

Jack cursed, and was about to take his chances on the broken barrels, when he noticed a shaft of light shining down on the beam. He followed it up and saw that it was coming from a vent in the peak of the roof. If he could reach the vent he might be able to push it out and squeeze himself onto the roof. Outside there would still be a twenty-foot drop, but there might be something softer to land on than solid oak.

He climbed.

43

They arrived at the house just as the sun was setting and a wagonload of people was heading down to Durango.

Patricia slid out of the backseat, followed by Dr. Pavlov. She stared at the magnificent house, wondering if Joanne and Jack were inside—scared, confused, perhaps hurt. It was all she could do to stop herself from running through the front door, screaming their names, and searching every room.

"Howdy, ma'am."

Startled, she turned. A man on a tall black horse loomed above her.

"Didn't mean to rile you," he said, tipping his hat, although he didn't look at all sorry. "My name is Raphael Aznar."

Patricia knew this before he said his name. Neil had described him perfectly, from the black mustache to the potbelly bulging over his fancy silver-studded gun belt. He swung off the stallion with surprising grace and agility, considering his bulk.

"And you are?" he said.

"Nicole Glaze," Patricia said. Another name change, but this one was *very* temporary.

Raphael frowned, clearly unfamiliar with the name. "And you?" He pointed at Dr. Pavlov, who was paying a lot more attention to the wagon making its way down to Durango than to the man with the horse.

"Pavlov," he said. "Dr. Igor Pavlov." He pointed at the limo. "I am Mr. Nile's personal physician. Miss Glaze is Mr. Nile's nurse."

Up to that moment, Patricia didn't know that Pavlov spoke English.

Raphael smiled for the first time since riding up. He had never met Mr. Nile, but he knew the name. He was a wealthy real estate developer that Alonzo had been trying to bring into the organization for years. They needed legitimate businesses where they could hide or launder their huge drug profits. What Raphael didn't know was that Mr. Nile could not walk.

The driver popped the car's trunk, pulled the wheelchair out, and pushed it around to the side. Raphael handed Diablo's reins to a servant and followed the driver.

An old man was sitting in the backseat.

"I'm Raphael Aznar."

Sam nodded without comment.

"I'm happy to see that you and your people dressed appropriately."

200

"I like a good costume party," Sam said.

"There is a slight problem, though."

"What's that?"

"Your wheelchair."

Sam stared at him.

"We allow nothing into Durango that did not exist in 1871."

"Nicole!" Sam shouted.

Patricia hurried around the limo, followed by Dr. Pavlov moving at a much more leisurely pace.

"Apparently, we're not welcome here," Sam said to her. "We're leaving."

"What?" Patricia could not disguise her dismay.

Sam ignored her and looked at Raphael, his face flushed in anger. "Your brother has been begging me to come down here for five years. I finally come, ready to do business, and I'm told I can't participate because I don't have the right wheelchair? It's outrageous."

Raphael didn't know what to do, but he did know what Alonzo would say if Mr. Nile left before a deal was struck. Backing off was not something Raphael was good at, and he cursed himself for bringing the wheelchair problem up in the first place.

It had been a bad day all the way around, and it was getting worse. Ten minutes after he talked to Zita in the library, he was told that the country band he had hired to entertain them had been arrested for drug possession in San Diego. The idiots. Why would anyone bring drugs to a drug dealer's house?

"Let's go," Sam said.

Patricia started to push the empty wheelchair back to the trunk, wondering what Sam was going to do now. She guessed he would hand it over to Neil.

"Wait," Raphael said. "Please. I'm being ridiculous. Of course we want you to stay. We will make an exception. I—" Raphael hesitated. "I apologize."

Sam gave him a reluctant nod.

"In fact," Raphael continued, "if you give me a few minutes, I'll ride down to Durango with you and make certain my men let you in without further trouble. You'll be more comfortable riding in the limo down to town. I have something to take care of in the house. I'll be right back. "

"Fine," Sam said.

Raphael walked up to the house. The apology stuck in his throat like an ice cube. He blamed Zita for this. He had been down at Durango taking care of last-minute details when he was told that she was at the house and needed to speak to him immediately. An emergency, the runner had said. If she hadn't sent the runner for him, he would have heard about the man in the wheelchair from one of his men and would have had more time to think about what to do. By the time he got through the front door he was furious. He found Zita sitting in the library.

"I have the girl," she said.

Raphael's anger disappeared. "And the boy?"

"Not yet," Zita answered. "But we'll have him soon."

He called one of the servants into the library and told him to escort Mr. Nile and his party to Durango. "Tell them that I have to take care of some last-minute details and that

I'll see them down there. Make certain the guards let the wheelchair through."

The servant nodded and left. Raphael turned back to Zita. "Now, tell me where you're keeping her."

44

Jack managed to get the roof vent out, but it took a lot of pounding. When it finally popped loose, it clattered down the metal roof like a machine gun going off.

He squeezed through the small opening, cutting his hand on the sharp metal edge, expecting to be surrounded by a bunch of cowboys standing below with pitchforks and pistols, but no one was waiting for him. He sat on the peak, catching his breath, watching the last of the sun disappear behind the Andes.

Now what? he thought. Two choices. I can walk to Mendoza, which would take all night, maybe longer, and try to find somebody to help me other than the police. Or, I can find Joanne, get her away from Snake Eyes, and we can try to stow away on one of the jets.

Neither of these choices were any good. If the police in Mendoza worked for the Aznars, it was likely that everyone in town was connected to them in some way. And the problem with the stowaway plan—aside from getting Joanne away from Snake Eyes, which seemed impossible at the moment—was that he had no idea where the jets were going. They could end up farther away from home than they already were.

He guessed that anywhere was better than here, and decided that if he couldn't find a way to spring Joanne, he would stow away by himself. When they landed, he would hope to be able to find someone to help.

The corrugated roof gave him a great view of the vineyard. He sat there for a few minutes studying the lay of the land so he would know where to go once he got down.

The house, where he figured Snake Eyes had taken Joanne, was on the hill above. All the lights were on. A group of people stood in the courtyard in front of a limo. Diablo was standing next to the car, held by a man who was clearly not Raphael Aznar. He was much shorter than Raphael. This meant that Raphael was probably inside the house. And if Joanne was there too . . . He didn't want to think about what that might mean.

The people got into the limo and it pulled away, leaving the front of the house deserted, except for Diablo and the man holding his reins.

Jack followed the limo's progress down the steep road, where it stopped outside the Old West town. There were lights in the town, but they were dim, and he could just barely make out the shadows of people and horses moving between the clapboard buildings. He heard laughter and shouts, a piano began to play. A party, he thought. The jets had flown people in for a hoedown or something. Time to go.

His idea was to work his way down the roof and crawl along the edge until he saw something that wouldn't break his neck or legs when he landed on it. He'd had enough broken legs in his life.

The idea was good in theory, but fell apart in practice. As soon as he eased himself onto the steep pitch he started to slide. He lunged for the peak, missed it by a good two feet, and realized that he was not going to drop—he was going to be launched. He flipped over on his back, preferring to see where he was going. A second later, he ran out of roof.

45

Snake Eyes had dragged Joanne around to the back of the big house, through the kitchen, and past a half dozen women preparing food, who didn't even look up from their work as they went by.

She pulled Joanne into a narrow hallway, then pushed her through a door leading to a set of steep stairs. At the bottom was a media room with at least two dozen comfortable chairs facing a large white viewing screen. She hit a button and the screen rolled up, revealing a hidden door. She pushed Joanne inside and slammed the door behind her. The lock snapped into place.

The room was pitch black. Joanne felt along the wall, and after several frantic minutes, fumbled onto the light switch with a sigh of relief.

The suite was similar to the one beneath the barn, but smaller, with only one bedroom. It was decorated in the same cowboy motif, which reminded her of Raphael and his promised visit. She shuddered with dread and revulsion.

If only Jack hadn't gotten claustrophobic, she thought, then shook the ill feeling off. He couldn't help himself, and if she hadn't tried out for *American SuperStar*, they would both be in L.A. right now. She just hoped he would head to Mendoza and not do something stupid like trying to rescue her. Mendoza was their only chance. But if they caught him on the way, or in town . . . She didn't want to think about that.

She went into the kitchen and opened the cupboards. Like the cupboards in the room beneath the barn, they were well stocked with food. If she was careful she could survive for weeks.

Survive, she thought. That's what I need to do. Survive long enough for someone to figure out where I am and rescue me. Keep the panic down. Think. I'll go back to my original plan. Block the door so they can't get in, like Jack did when he trapped the woman in the bathroom. What did Jack say? "They'll cut the power and water. . . ." I can survive the dark, but I can't live without water.

She filled every container in the cupboard with water, and was on her way into the bathroom to fill the bathtub . . .

When the door opened.

She let out an involuntary shriek.

Raphael smiled at her reaction. Snake Eyes regarded her grimly through purple contacts, which were scarier than her previous pair.

"Sit down," Raphael said.

208

Joanne fought back her rising panic by taking a deep breath and letting it out slowly. If she were to survive she would have to keep her wits about her, she would have to think. She sat down in the chair rather than the sofa, so Raphael could not sit next to her.

The woman went into the kitchen and came out with a pitcher filled with water.

"Thirsty?" she said with an evil smile.

Joanne did not respond.

"Or perhaps," the woman continued, "you were thinking of blocking the door from the inside and staying here until someone came to your rescue?"

Joanne frowned, but it wasn't because they had discovered her plan. She was angry because she should have blocked the door first and waited on the water. Jack would have thought of that.

She looked at Raphael. He was still smiling, and she noticed for the first time that he was carrying something draped over his arm. It looked like a red dress.

"I understand," he drawled, "that your voice is as pretty as you are."

Joanne shrugged. The woman walked back into the kitchen. Joanne could hear her emptying the water into the sink.

"Do you sing country?" Raphael asked.

Joanne stared at him. "Why?" she asked.

"We got ourselves a li'l situation here," he said. "We're having ourselves a jamboree down in Durango and our entertainment didn't arrive. Thought you'd like to fill in for them."

"You've got to be kidding," Joanne said.

Raphael shook his head. "The way I figure it," he said. "It would be a sight better down in Durango than shut up all by your lonesome here."

He had a point, but she couldn't believe that, after kidnapping and threatening to kill them, he would think that she would actually sing for him and his dope-dealing friends. He was crazier than he looked.

"Well?" he said.

"No." It was out before she knew what she was saying.

A frown crossed Raphael's face. "Figured you might feel that way, and that's a shame. You see . . ." He looked at Snake Eyes, who had walked back into the room. "We have your brother."

The smile had returned to Raphael's face. Joanne looked at Snake Eyes. She looked annoyed.

"Where is he?"

"Safe," Raphael said. "For now. We have him locked up under the barn. Thought it best to keep you two separated. Zita was all for killing him. Truth be told, I was too, but then I started thinking about the jamboree. . . ."

"Where did you find him?" Joanne asked, wondering if they really did have him.

"He didn't make it far," Raphael said.

"I want to see him."

Raphael shook his head. "You have yourself two choices. You sing for my friends or I send Zita over to take care of your brother. And believe me, she's real eager to get the job done."

"And if I sing?"

"Then your brother will live," Raphael said. "But you must cooperate. No trying to get away. No telling my guests who you really are. Zita will be keeping an eye on you every second. If you mess up, she'll kill both of you."

"Can I see him after I sing?" Joanne asked.

"Depends on how you sing. You do a good job, we might arrange a reunion." He dropped the red dress on her lap. "Slip it on."

46

It was like stepping back in time. Durango not only looked and sounded like the Old West, it smelled like the Old West. Or what Patricia imagined the Old West smelled like—wood smoke, tobacco, mud, dung, sawdust—pungent, but not altogether unpleasant.

As Sam had anticipated, they were searched before being let into the town, but the guards did not find the wheelchair's two-way radio or the taser gun concealed in Dr. Pavlov's medical bag.

With some difficulty, Patricia pushed Sam's wheelchair across the rutted street to the boardwalk where the pushing got easier.

Sam switched on the two-way and said quietly, "Do you copy?"

"Loud and clear." Neil's voice answered into the earpiece.

"We're in Durango, heading to the saloon for the meeting. Stand by."

"Roger."

Neil looked at Smitty in relief.

"So far so good," Smitty said.

They were dressed in assault vests, night-vision goggles, throat radios that could be heard at a whisper, stocking caps—everything camouflaged, including their faces.

The plan was simple: Sam, Patricia, and Pavlov would subdue Raphael during their one-on-one meeting with him. They would find out where Jack and Joanne were being held. Neil and Smitty would free the kids and take them back to the jet. When the kids were safely on board, Patricia, Sam, and Pavlov would leave Durango, join them on the jet, and they would take off.

As simple as the plan was, Neil knew that a lot could still go wrong. They would have less than half an hour with Raphael in the room before his security people got suspicious. The Aznars did not waste time in meetings. The other problem was they had no idea when Sam would be called into the room. Neil hoped it was a little later in the evening so he and Smitty would have time to reconnoiter. He wanted more than one escape route back to the jet in case they ran into trouble.

"We got everything?" Smitty asked.

Neil took one last look around and saw Commander IF between the pilot and copilot seat. He put the figure in his pocket.

47

Raphael did not have Jack.

Although he could have, had he or any of his people wandered around to the side of the building. Jack had landed on his back, hit his head, and everything went black.

It was a good five or six minutes before his eyelids began to flicker open. At first he thought he was below his bedroom window at his old house, where he had taken his famous leap in his sister's red tights and a sheet tied around his neck like a superhero. But where was the grape arbor? He felt his neck. Where was the sheet? He felt his legs. Where were the tights?

He tried to sit up, but the pain was too intense. He lay still and stared up at the bright stars in the night sky. Slowly it all came back to him.

He grabbed a handful of what he had landed on and brought it up to his face. Sawdust. He had landed on a pile of sawdust from the barrels. He tried to sit up again, and made it this time, but it felt like every bone in his body was broken. He had to get up to the house. Joanne was there.

Shakily, he got to his feet and realized that something really was broken, or at least badly sprained. His right ankle was the color of a ripe plum and twice as big as his left. He took a tentative step and sucked in his breath. It was bad, but he could walk.

•

48

Patricia, Sam, and Dr. Pavlov sat around an old table in the Aznar Saloon.

The floor was covered in sawdust and the air was thick with smoke. The jamboree was in full swing. People were drinking, playing cards, and practicing their quick draw out on the street. Every time a gun went off, Patricia jumped. Sam and Dr. Pavlov didn't even blink.

Three groups had already been in and out of the back room with Raphael. The fourth group was in there now. They weren't staying inside nearly as long as Sam wanted.

"When do you think he'll call us in?" Patricia said.

Sam shrugged. "We're ready whenever he is."

Patricia didn't know what he meant by this, but a few minutes earlier Dr. Pavlov had wheeled him out back to use the outhouse. When they came back in Sam had a small blanket over his lap. She was as nervous as she had ever been, and hoped it didn't show.

Finally the door opened. Raphael came out smiling, clapping his two visitors on the back. He walked over to the long mahogany bar with them, got a beer, then walked over to their table.

"Mr. Nile, y'all ready to come into the back and have a palaver?"

"Fine."

Patricia and Dr. Pavlov started to get up.

"Our business is with you, Mr. Nile, not your medical staff. I can push you in."

"Then we're not going to do business," Sam said. "I don't go anywhere without them. This is not just my medical staff. They are my partners. We have no secrets."

Raphael looked at them a moment, then shrugged. "Come on, then."

"They're in," Neil said, waving Smitty to a stop.

They were slowly working their way toward the house. So far, they had not run into a single guard or any security. It seemed that everyone was down at Durango, which would suit their mission perfectly, provided that Joanne and Jack were being held somewhere on the vineyard and not in Durango.

They crouched behind the barn and listened to the conversation between Raphael Aznar and Mr. Nile.

49

It took Jack a long time to hobble his way up to the house. His ankle throbbed, sending stabs of shooting pain all the way up to his neck, but he finally made it.

He stood outside for several minutes, trying to decide what to do. Diablo was gone, which meant that Raphael was at the Old West town. At least, Jack hoped he was down there.

His instinct told him to limp down to the airfield as fast as he could and climb aboard one of the jets while everyone was partying. But his conscience was telling him something else. He couldn't get over the image of Joanne waving good-bye behind her back as Snake Eyes led her out of the building. Even if it meant getting caught, he had to try to find her.

He limped through the front door of the house.

Zita was furious at Raphael.

Using the girl to entertain the guests was insane. If

Alonzo were here, or even in touch, he would have never allowed it. She had written him a dozen e-mails and had gotten nothing in return. Something was seriously wrong, and this was another reason she was mad at Raphael. He didn't seem to care.

She and the girl were across the street from the saloon, at the dry goods store, going over the music she was to sing, with Raphael's piano player. Zita had been demoted to translator, and this was the third thing she was angry about.

"You've rehearsed enough," Zita said. "Let's get this over with."

That was fine with Joanne. The sooner it was over, the sooner she could see Jack. She and the piano player followed Zita out of the store.

Raphael took his seat behind a huge antique oak desk with a green blotter on top. The dim gaslights hissed behind him.

"What do ya'll think of Durango?" he asked.

"Impressive," Sam said.

Raphael's eye drifted over to Patricia, who was standing to the right of the wheelchair. Pavlov stood to the left. "And how 'bout you, Miss Glaze?"

"It's like stepping back into—"

There was a loud *pop!* Raphael's chair slammed into the wall. His eyes went wide and he began to convulse. Sam and Pavlov were up and behind the desk in a flash. Sam slapped a gag over Raphael's mouth, tore the two taser probes from his chest, and slipped the six-shooters out of his holsters. He then took a small digital camera out of his pocket and nodded at Dr. Pavlov.

Pavlov pulled an odd-looking syringe out of his bag, pushed Raphael's head to the side, and injected him in the neck.

"Truth serum?" Patricia asked.

"No," Sam said as he continued to take photographs. "It's a heart attack pill. Lock the door, please. We don't want any unexpected guests."

Confused, Patricia quietly twisted the skeleton key in the old lock. When she turned back around, Dr. Pavlov was pointing a small electronic instrument at Raphael's chest.

"It's in place," he said.

Sam nodded. He pushed Raphael into the corner and pulled his chair up in front of him. He re-armed the stun gun and pointed it inches from Raphael's chest. Raphael had come to, and was staring at Sam in defiant rage. His rage turned to horror when Sam started speaking in perfectly accented Spanish.

Patricia did not understand what he was saying, but it was clear from Raphael's expression that it was terrifying him.

"Are you getting any of this?" Smitty asked. He didn't speak Spanish.

Neil held his finger up to his lips. Sam was away from the wheelchair, and it was taking all of Neil's concentration to piece together the conversation. He had learned enough to know that he never wanted to get on the wrong side of Sam Sebesta and Dr. Igor Pavlov. What Sam was explaining to Raphael was as simple as it was diabolical.

50

Jack was relieved to find the house deserted. He decided to start at the top and work his way down, checking every room.

Raphael's bedroom took up almost half of the top floor, and it was locked. But thanks to Snake Eyes, Jack had a key. He stepped into the walk-in closet and flipped on the light. It was filled with rack after rack of western clothes, cowboy hats, and dozens of pairs of cowboy boots.

Next to the closet was another door. Locked. Jack opened it hopefully, but Joanne wasn't there. Inside were hundreds of antique weapons—Winchesters, Sharpes, Colts—some were displayed in glass cases, others hung on the wall. He took a Colt revolver down. It was heavy. He snapped open the cylinder. It was loaded. He slipped it under his belt and continued his search.

Raphael was shaking now.

Sam reached into his pocket and took out what looked like a small remote control. The kind used for automatically locking and unlocking a car. There was a single red button on it.

"Remove the gag," he said.

Dr. Pavlov tore the duct tape away.

Sam held the remote inches from Raphael's face, with his thumb poised over the red button. "One chance, Raphael," he said in English. "Tell me where the children are."

Sweat poured down Raphael's face. "The girl is here. I don't know where the boy is. He—"

Someone beyond the door had started singing.

"That's Joanne!" Patricia cried.

"I recognize the voice," Sam said, then turned to Raphael. "Let's go." He showed him the remote. "If anything happens to her, you're dead."

Raphael got up from the chair shakily.

When Zita led Joanne into the saloon, no one paid any attention to her. They were too busy laughing, playing cards, and drinking. They certainly didn't look like drug dealers.

She went over the order of the songs with the piano player.

"Ready?"

"*Sí.*"

The piano player started to play and Joanne started to sing. At first no one seemed to care, then, one by one, people put their drinks down, stopped talking, and turned toward the piano. She was a third of the way through the first song when a door near the end of the bar burst open.

A pretty woman with short black hair came out and stared at her. Joanne continued to sing. The woman started walking toward her. Halfway across the saloon she started to run toward her.

Joanne stopped singing. The woman looked like—

Joanne dropped the microphone and stepped off the small stage.

Zita grabbed her arm and viciously wrenched it behind her back. She put a small derringer against her head, glaring at Patricia. "Another step and I kill her!"

"No!" Patricia slid to a stop.

"Mom?"

"Let her go, Zita!" Raphael shouted. Standing next to him was a little man with thick glasses—and Sam Sebesta.

"What's going on?" Joanne asked.

"Shut up!" Zita twisted her arm farther.

Joanne screamed.

"For the love of God, Zita, let her go," Raphael pleaded.

Zita shook her head.

"They'll kill me."

Zita laughed. "If I let her go, your brother will rot in prison forever. That's what you want, isn't it?"

"No, it isn't."

The people in the saloon were looking back and forth between Zita and Raphael in utter confusion.

Zita started dragging Joanne toward the door.

"Don't follow, or I swear I'll kill her right here."

"You won't get off the vineyard, Zita," Raphael said. "The guards will stop you. Give it up."

Zita shook her head and backed out through the swinging saloon doors.

By this time, several of the guests had unholstered their guns and were shouting at Raphael in English and in Spanish.

"Zita has gone loco," Raphael said.

Many of them knew Zita and they didn't seem surprised.

"Everyone stay here. Enjoy yourselves. I will take care of it."

Sam hurried back into the room to get the hidden radio from the wheelchair.

As soon as they heard Patricia scream Joanne's name, Neil and Smitty left the shelter of the barn and started running toward Durango. They were halfway down the road to the town when a wagon rushed passed them. Smitty snapped his rifle up and aimed at the driver, but he wasn't sure who it was. He didn't take the shot.

"Are you there?" Sam's voice came over their headsets.

"Yeah. What's happening? A wagon just came up the hill like a bat out of—"

"That was Joanne."

Neil swore.

"Where's Jack?"

"Unknown. The woman's armed. She'll kill Joanne if—"

Neil and Smitty started running up the road, chasing the wagon toward the house.

51

By the time Jack got down to the basement, he was very discouraged. No sign of Joanne. There was a media room down there, with all the latest equipment.

He sat down in one of the leather chairs to rest his leg for a minute, and thought about what he should do. It would take him days to search the vineyard, and his ankle was getting worse. If he didn't start for the airfield soon, he might not make it.

He got up and was about to drag his leg outside, when he noticed that the movie screen was not pulled all the way down. He stared at the screen for a second and saw the bottom of a door behind it. He raised the screen and discovered the secret room. Joanne's clothes were strewn on the floor.

Zita held the derringer in one hand and the reins in the other as the wagon clattered up the road at breakneck speed.

Joanne thought about jumping, but the wagon was going too fast. Even if she managed to land without breaking anything, she was sure Snake Eyes would catch her. Part of her western outfit included a pair of boots that were at least a size too small for her.

She was still bewildered at seeing her mom and Sam Sebesta in the saloon. What were they doing there? How had they gotten there? And why hadn't Zita let her go when Raphael told her to?

The wagon nearly ran over a couple of people on the road. Joanne turned and saw one of them bring his rifle up to his shoulder, but they rounded the corner before he could shoot.

Zita pulled back viciously on the reins in front of the house, causing the team to rear.

"If you resist I will shoot you right here!" she said, holding the derringer against Joanne's chest.

"What are we doing?"

"Shut up! No talking!"

She yanked Joanne off the wagon and pulled her into the house. They passed through the entryway and down the hall. When they reached the door leading down to the media room, Zita pushed her down the stairs. The door to the secret room was wide open.

"Get in there!"

Joanne got up and scrambled inside, thinking that Zita would slam the door behind her. But instead, Zita followed her in and locked the door behind both of them. She put the derringer in her pocket and glared around the room wildly. She grabbed a chair and wedged it under the doorknob.

226

"Go into the kitchen and refill those containers with water," she shouted. "We're going to be here for a while."

Jack stepped out of the bedroom. He was holding the pistol with two hands, the hammer cocked all the way back.

"Get away from the door," he said, with a quivering voice.

Zita smiled. "Your hand is shaking." She reached for the derringer.

Jack squeezed the trigger. There was a deafening explosion. Joanne screamed. The room filled with gun smoke. Zita was several feet away from the door, holding her leg.

"Let's get out of here!" Jack shouted, but he could barely hear himself above the ringing in his ears.

"Mom . . ." Joanne said. "Sam Sebesta . . ."

Jack tried to clear his ears. "What did you—"

The door blew off its hinges. Two men burst through the opening in full tactical gear, carrying assault rifles. They pointed them at Zita in deadly silence, then flipped her over and put plastic cuffs on her wrists.

Smitty broke into a bright smile. "Hi, Jacko."

Neil crossed over and hugged his children.

Minutes later, Patricia rushed into the room, followed by Sam, Dr. Pavlov, and Raphael. They had driven the limo up to the house.

"Thank God!" She grabbed Jack and Joanne as if she would never let them go.

Jack was still in a state of shock at seeing his parents and Sam, and the funny little man with the thick glasses examining Zita's leg.

"How did you get here?"

"We'll have plenty of time to tell you on the flight home," Neil said.

"Home!" Patricia said.

Neil looked at Raphael and nodded. He and Smitty's assault rifles were still at the ready in case something happened.

Raphael looked pale and shaken. He kept glancing nervously at Sam. Snake Eyes was grimacing in pain. Jack thought that he would feel bad about having shot her, but the truth was, he didn't. She would have killed him and Joanne if she had gotten the chance.

"I'll stabilize the leg," Dr. Pavlov said to Raphael. "But you'll have to get her to a hospital."

"Make it quick, Doc," Smitty said. "We have a flight to catch."

It took Dr. Pavlov only a few minutes. When he finished he took his odd-looking syringe out of his bag and gave her a shot in the neck.

Raphael grimaced.

Snake Eyes glowered at Pavlov. "What did you just give me?"

"A condition," Pavlov answered. "Raphael will tell you all about it."

"We're outta here," Neil said. "Smitty will lead the way. I'll take up the rear."

Jack took a step forward and winced in pain.

"What's the matter, Jack?" Patricia asked.

"Sprained ankle," he said.

Dr. Pavlov lifted his pant leg and shook his head. "Not sprained. Broken."

"We'll drive the limo to the airfield," Sam said.

Neil handed his rifle to Sam. "You carry this. I'll carry Jack."

"I can walk," Jack protested.

Neil shook his head. "I'm carrying you." He grinned. "End of subject."

Jack grinned back at him.

As they filed out of the room, Sam looked at Raphael and said, "We'll be watching."

Raphael blanched another shade paler.

Day Six

THE HOSPITAL

52

They flew all night.

Three black SUVs were waiting for them at the Atlanta airport, driven by very serious and athletic-looking men in nice suits.

When they got to the hospital, there were some familiar faces waiting for them in the emergency room. Marshals Doris Welty and Donald Smites and Agent Pelton from the Drug Enforcement Agency were there along with another man who Jack didn't recognize. He was tall and fat, and wore rose-tinted eyeglasses.

The man looked at Jack's father and mother. "I'm sorry for all your troubles. It was nothing personal."

Neil gave him a hard look. Sam put a restraining hand on Neil's arm and said, "He's on our side now."

Neil's expression did not soften.

The man smiled at Sam and Dr. Pavlov. "How many years has it been?"

Neil raised his voice. "You know each other?"

Sam nodded and looked at Patricia. "This is a colleague of Igor's and mine from our cold war days. Back then he was known as Alexander Petrovich, but you know him as El Sereno, or The Watcher."

Patricia's expression turned as hard as Neil's. Jack thought for a second that she might slap him. Doris and Don's expressions were sour as well.

"It seems that he was right in Atlanta, doing what he does best," Sam explained. "I called him from the plane on our way to Argentina. I asked him to come over to our side and, seeing that he was about to lose his current job, he agreed. We need someone with his talents. He introduced himself to the marshals and invited them to meet us at the hospital."

A young emergency room doctor came over and looked at Jack, who was sitting in a wheelchair. "You must be the one with the broken ankle."

Jack nodded. During the flight Dr. Pavlov had stabilized the ankle as best he could and given him some painkillers, but it was still throbbing.

"We'll get you into X-ray, then see what we can do about putting you back together."

"While you're getting fixed up," Sam said, "we're going to visit another patient."

"Who?" Jack asked.

"I'll tell you later," Sam said, patting his shoulder.

Neil reached into his pocket and pulled Commander IF out. "I believe this is yours."

Jack was as surprised to see Commander IF as his father

234

was to learn that Sam knew El Sereno. The tiny astronaut was scarred and beaten up, as if it had been to Mars and back. Just like me, he thought. "Where did you get him?"

"Catalin gave him to me," Neil said. "She said she thought you could use a friend, but it's just a loan. She wants Commander IF back."

"Does that mean I can see her again?"

Patricia smiled. "I think that can be arranged."

The doctor wheeled him away. Joanne and Patricia followed.

53

"You're not my regular doctor," Alonzo Aznar said.

"That is correct." The doctor looked at Alonzo's chart. "I'm a specialist."

"When am I getting out of here?"

"Very soon, I think," the doctor said. "But first I need to examine you."

Alonzo had been poked, prodded, and probed by a half dozen doctors in the past few days, and he was thoroughly sick of it. No one would tell him anything. His sense of dread had been building, and he was frightened, an emotion he was not very familiar with.

Bender had not come to see him that day, nor had he returned his calls. And there was still no word from Raphael, Zita, or El Sereno.

The doctor had his back to Alonzo and was taking something out of his bag.

"What kind of specialist are you?" Alonzo asked, with the spider-like sensation moving up his spine.

"I'm a heart specialist," the doctor said, turning around with a stun gun in his hand.

Alonzo lunged from the bed, but he was too late.

When Alonzo came to, he found himself gagged with a swatch of duct tape and he was tied down to the bed. Standing next to the bed were Neil Osborne, Sam Sebesta, and the doctor who had shot him. He tried to free himself, but the bonds held fast.

Sam waited for him to stop struggling, then said in a very quiet and level voice, "You need to listen to me very carefully."

Alonzo stared at him with bulging eyes.

"Do you know who I am?"

Alonzo nodded.

"You know Neil Osborne, of course."

Alonzo looked at Neil and didn't like what he saw there. Neil was grinning at him.

"And this man," Sam said, nodding toward Igor, "is Dr. Pavlov."

Of the three of them, Dr. Pavlov was perhaps the most frightening. He looked down at Alonzo with completely dead eyes, as if he were observing a laboratory rat he was about to sacrifice.

"Now that we have the introductions taken care of," Sam continued, "I am going to remove the gag. This wing of the hospital has been emptied. If you yell out, people will come through the door, but you should know that none of them like you very much. They will not help you." He tore the duct tape off.

"Let me tell what has happened to you. You did not have a heart attack in jail. We gave you a drug to simulate a heart attack so we could get you into the hospital."

Alonzo thought about what he was going do to the inmate who had slipped him the poisoned food.

"While you were here this week," Sam continued, "we were down in Argentina. Jack and Joanne are safe."

Alonzo thought Sam was bluffing. He believed that the whole thing was a setup to get him to tell them where the kids were. "I don't know what you're talking about," he said.

Sam smiled. "I thought you might say that." He picked up a manila envelope and opened it. "I know you are fond of digital photography. I've seen some of your work. Here's some of mine."

He held up a series of photos of the Osborne family aboard the jet.

"You are probably familiar with this airplane," Sam said. "It belongs to you, or it did. We borrowed it to fly down and get the children. And we are going to keep it. Along with everything else you own that's useful to us."

He took out some more photographs.

"Now, these next photographs will be of particular interest to you, I think."

He showed him photos of a very frightened Raphael Aznar tied to a chair.

"Raphael!" Alonzo said.

"He's alive," Sam said. "At least for now. Whether

he stays alive is completely up to you."

"What do you mean?"

Sam showed him another picture. Dr. Pavlov was injecting something into Raphael's neck.

"What are you doing to him?" Alonzo shouted.

"The same thing we just did to you," Sam said. "Is your neck sore?"

Alonzo's neck *was* throbbing. He tried to feel the sore spot, but couldn't because his hands were tied. He started to tremble.

"Dr. Pavlov," Sam said, "was telling the truth when he told you that he was a heart specialist. He specializes in *causing* heart attacks, not preventing them. You have been injected with a microscopic radio-activated capsule, undetectable and unremovable. It will float freely in your body, migrating here and there for the rest of your life." Sam took a small remote control out of his pocket. "Do you see this red button?"

Alonzo nodded fearfully.

"If I press this button, that capsule in your body will explode. Approximately seventy seconds later your heart will stop working and no CPR, no surgeon, no medication will get it going again. To put it simply. You will die."

"You're lying," Alonzo said.

"I'll just press this button and we'll see."

"No!" Alonzo said, sweat pouring off his face.

Sam tossed the remote control to Neil.

Neil caught it and smiled. "Adios, Alonzo." He put his thumb over the red button.

"Please, Neil, no!"

Neil hesitated.

"You have a heart condition now, Alonzo," Sam said, his expression deadly serious. "So does your brother. And so does Zita. We could have killed you in jail. We could have killed Raphael and Zita in Argentina. But we've chosen to let you live, for the time being. And here are the conditions. Listen very carefully, because if you or your brother or Zita violate one of these conditions, the red button will be pushed. Do you believe me?"

Alonzo nodded.

"Your cartel is finished," Sam said. "Thanks to Neil's diary, the United States Government has frozen all of your assets and confiscated everything you own in this country. As I'm talking to you right now, your home in Colombia and all your drug factories and warehouses are being burned to the ground. If you sell another ounce of drugs, you and your brother and Zita will have simultaneous heart attacks. Do you understand?"

Again, Alonzo nodded.

"You will not pursue the Osbornes or anyone else you have a vendetta toward. In other words, if you or your brother or Zita harm another living being, you will all pay for it with your lives. Do you understand?"

"Yes," Alonzo managed to say.

"Finally, the federal prosecutors have offered you a plea bargain. You will take their offer. With good behavior, and providing you don't have a heart attack in prison, you will be out in five years. You will be deported to Argentina to join your brother on the vineyard, which we have spared. And there you will stay for the rest of your life. Do you understand?"

"Yes."

"You are probably thinking that you will be able to figure a way out of this, or that we will tire of watching you." Sam shook his head. "Get that idea out of your mind. You and Raphael will be watched every second of every day by someone who you know can do that job."

El Sereno stepped out of the shadows into the light.

54

"So that's what happened," Jack said. He handed Commander IF to Catalin Cristobal. "I think this is yours."

"I think he belongs to both of us," Cat said, taking the battered astronaut.

They were sitting in Sam Sebesta's old room at the Nevada Hotel in Elko. Jack had his leg propped up on the bed. The desert sunlight coming through the window was beginning to fade. They had been in the room for hours talking.

"Do you think there is really some kind of heart attack pill?" Cat asked.

Jack smiled. "I don't know. But Alonzo and Raphael believe there is."

"And Alonzo took the plea bargain?"

Jack nodded. "He started his prison term two days ago."

"What about Sam?" Cat asked. "What's he up to?"

Jack shook his head. "That's still a big mystery. I think he had more than just saving us in mind when he put this all together."

"What do you mean?"

"He wants my parents to come work for him."

"Doing what?"

"I'm not sure," Jack said. "Going after bad guys. I think it has to do with terrorism. All I know is that my parents are talking about it. Whatever they decide to do, they won't do it until after we find out if Joanne makes the *American SuperStar* finals."

"And you'll stay here until then?"

Jack smiled. "If it's okay with you."

Catalin kissed him.

Jack pulled an envelope out of his pocket and gave it to her. In it was the letter he had always wanted to send to her, but couldn't.